THE LOVE-HATE RELATION

THE LOVE-HATE
RELATION

John Newton Chance

CHIVERS
THORNDIKE

This Large Print book is published by BBC Audiobooks Ltd, Bath, England and by Thorndike Press®, Waterville, Maine, USA.

Published in 2005 in the U.K. by arrangement with Robert Hale Limited.
Published in 2005 in the U.S. by arrangement with Robert Hale Limited.

U.K. Hardcover   ISBN 1–4056–3154–6 (Chivers Large Print)
U.K. Softcover   ISBN 1–4056–3155–4 (Camden Large Print)
U.S. Softcover   ISBN 0–7862–7016–0 (Nightingale)

The text of this Large Print edition is unabridged.
Other aspects of the book may vary from the original edition.

Set in 16 pt. New Times Roman.

Printed in Great Britain on acid-free paper.

British Library Cataloguing in Publication Data available

Library of Congress Cataloging-in-Publication Data

Chance, John Newton.
   The love-hate relation / by John Newton Chance.
      p.   cm.
   ISBN 0–7862–7016–0 (lg. print : sc : alk. paper)
   1. Large type books. I. Title.
PR6005.H28L687 2004
823'.912—dc22   2004057989

CHAPTER ONE

1

At 11.15 p.m. on the night of January fifteenth Philip Stanley suddenly had the feeling that he was being followed. The night was misty, the wet dripping from the staring naked trees over the path across the common. In the distance the lights strung along Fairfield Avenue hung in the mist like floating moons with many rings. The path was hard under his feet, but his soft shoes made little sound.

At the outset, when the feeling came that somebody was in the misty dark behind him, he thought that perhaps guilt was stirring phantoms of feeling in his mind, bringing the ghost of Nemesis who wasn't there. But it was too strong a feeling to be caused by a strained imagination.

As he walked the path without looking back, he tried to hear the sound of someone behind. The plopping of the wet from the naked branches overhead spoilt the concentration of his hearing and rattled out everything that might have been there to hear.

He slowed down as if at last his hours of tension, his wound-up resolve to go ahead with his work, was dragging him back. The house was not far ahead then, but if somebody walked behind, watching, then it could not be done that night. Perhaps it could not be done any night.

But it was only on that night the circumstances were right for Philip Stanley. The murder at any other time could not succeed in its purpose.

Several times he thought he heard a step shielding behind the spattering curtain of noise from the wet, but it was not sound he was going by. It was the feeling, the sense of no longer being alone on that desolate winter common.

Fear rose in a peak suddenly. He thought of turning and running back, shoving the follower aside into the drenched bushes beside the path and running on, back to the car so far behind him now. And once in it he would drive away, escape . . .

To where? Where now?

He almost stopped on the path and the answer whispered in his brain.

'There is nowhere now. It is too late. The bridge behind is down.'

He pulled a coin from the pocket of his coat and dropped it on the path. It clinked. He stopped, turned and pretended to look for it with a pealight on his car key fob. The wet dripped on, monotonous, deliberate.

Then he heard someone moving. It was a strange sound, a shuffling, but regular as footsteps of a sort he did not place for a moment.

The sound went off, drawing away in the mist to his right, he thought he saw a dark patch in the thin drizzling mist, going along on the other side of the trees. The sound was of shoes brushing through grass. It seemed to fade, draw farther away, and then stop altogether.

Stanley snicked off the light and put it back in his pocket. In the cold night his face felt clammy, even hot.

The lights of the Avenue glowed through the mist.

Of course, it could have been anybody coming home latish, walking so far along the path, then taking a short cut across the Common to his house in the Avenue.

It could have been. But if it had, why had the sounds stopped?

He listened to the dismal plopping of the wet, closed his eyes and felt the cold damp on his lashes, and for a moment his sight was misted when he opened them again and he felt a sudden surge of panic that he was being cheated of seeing his follower clearly.

A tremor ran through his nerves. He took off his hat and wiped his face with a handkerchief already damp from mopping sweat. When he put on his hat again he looked at his watch, a green dot circle in the dark.

Eleven-thirty. He had been frightened of the follower for fifteen minutes.

He looked around in the mist, then braced his shoulders. It must be now or never at all. The man in the mist was a genuine late night home-goer, short cutting over the Common. It had to be.

Stanley went on at last. When he came to the fork in the path he took the left. The big trees overhead kept plopping wet on to the tarmac, and the brief dry marks of Stanley's shoes faded behind him into the uniform wet blackness of the surface.

Some way down he stopped on the path close to where the great bole of an elm rose like a ghost in the misty wet. He looked round him. No sound but the water dripping.

He went off the path under the elm where no grass grew and the ground was hard. Beyond the tree the high black cliff of a garden wall ran away into nothing on either side of the lighter oblong of a door.

He went to it and turned the heavy handle. The door pushed in. Of course the door pushed in. The key was lost and the broken bolt at the bottom on the inside had still not been mended.

Philip Stanley stepped in, looked back once at the grey dripping scene, then closed the door.

4

Once, long ago, the Common had been the grounds of the house called Fairfield. Fairfield was built in 1850, in the middle of extensive grounds, by a Cornishman, Jeremy Isaacs, an inventor of great scope and greater success. On his death in 1890, he had left the Common as public land forever, but sold the house and all the land, more than forty yards in front of it. Gradually the outskirts of the town had been built on this land, reaching to the east side only of the Avenue named after the house, the West side being the open Common and the great, solitary house, like a fort behind its garden walls, close to the edge of it.

Fairfield was bought in 1892 by a Roger Borrow, founder of magazines and a large publishing house, and a very elegant life went on there until the first Great War, when one tragedy after another began a kind of spiritual rot.

In 1915 the eldest son Alan, returning from a business trip to New York was lost on the *Lusitania*. The only other child, Raymond, had joined the Royal Horse Artillery shortly before, and his mother's anxiety for him was suddenly capped by news of the *Lusitania*. She died in early 1916, everyone said from shock and sorrow.

In the German advance of Spring 1918, Raymond was killed fighting a rearguard action. Roger lived on at Fairfield alone, ageing, lost. Two years later he shot himself with a sporting gun.

During that War, Sebastian Stanley had set himself up as a manufacturer with a twenty pound loan with the object of avoiding any possible military call-up. Sharp to see where advantage lay, he got a contract for making small parts for webbing equipment, subbing to a large manufacturer. From there things grew from shed to huts, from huts to factory and the products were anything that the Government desperately needed to keep the Army and Navy in the field.

In 1918, when Sebastian had made a small fortune, his contracts were withdrawn and he was accused of supplying deliberately substandard goods, made with inferior materials which could not stand up to the purpose for which they were intended.

Enquiries took a long time. The War ended, the look-in dragged on and on. Legal action was prepared, and then, for a reason never explained, was dropped.

In 1920, Sebastian, fortune intact though reputation gone, bought Fairfield and settled in with many servants and a number of mistresses and boy friends, from whom he borrowed vast sums for various projects of his own and, for reasons which applied then, but perhaps not now, did not repay and the duped did nothing about it.

All this time his sister, who had married a man returning from the war, tried to get money she had lent for the original manufacturing ventures back from Sebastian, but failed to get through his excuses. In the end she turned her back on him, and that was the end of brother and sister in the family sense.

Several times Sebastian wrote when with projects which could, he said, get her money back for her, but she ignored the letters. Philip was born and for some years stayed in ignorance that he had an Uncle.

With the Second World War, Sebastian rushed back into manufacturing bits and pieces for a Government which didn't remember anything about the first fraudulent affair, until another case of back-doubling on a contract stirred some old files and his tap was stopped. But not before some new coffers had been stocked to a comforting solidity. This was desirable, for Sebastian was only as old as the century and able to enjoy things.

But after the war there were few servants to be got, and they got fewer so that life in Fairfield began to decay into a kind of elegant squalor. This increased until, with the passing years the shape and design of the house became the only grandeur left, and in his advancing years, Sebastian was attended by only a daily housekeeper.

Yet still he kept the outside front wall

painted and tidy. Still it appeared to be the House of a Master. Still Sebastian drove his 1939 Rolls where he wanted to go, for still he had the money, but for two reasons it would not work for him.

First, there was no labour; no servants anyhow, who wanted to go to him, no matter what the price. In the past too many had tried, and all of them had talked. Second, as he grew older so he grew afraid that his riches might suddenly dwindle and fade right away, leaving him to starve.

Sometimes he would sit alone in his once elegant drawing-room, drink Scotch until he cried because nobody cared about him.

The more selfish you become, the quicker you notice that people are getting too selfish to notice you. Sebastian became obsessed with this idea, and when he was suffering with special agony he would rush down to the end of his drive and throw things at people walking along the Avenue.

Twice he was hauled before the Magistrates for such assaults and carried out his own impassioned defence by shouting, 'Because they're a toffee-nosed lot of bastards and if they want to go about thinking I'm nothing I'll bloody soon shovel bloody showers of bloody . . .'

'Five pounds,' said the Chairman of the Bench. 'And costs.'

'. . . on top of 'em,' ended Sebastian in some

sort of strange triumph.

'Five pounds and costs,' repeated the Chairman.

'I'll go to prison!' shouted Sebastian.

'Are you sure you know what you're talking about?' asked the Chairman. 'This is only five pounds and costs, and you spent a good part of the morning telling us that you are being insulted as if you were a pauper.'

Something made Sebastian change his mind, and it was just that he was so proud of his position that he did not want a lot of strangers poking around his house while he was away.

'Time to pay!' cried Sebastian.

'The amount,' said the Clerk to the Justices, 'is in all only eight pounds sixteen. Do you mean to ask for time to pay such a sum as that?'

The public started laughing, particularly those waiting their turn to perform in the dock.

'Toffee-nosed lot of poops!' shouted Sebastian, bouncing up and down like an enraged gnome.

'We can send a bailiff round to take something of equal value . . .' began the Clerk.

'You send a bailiff round to me and I'll kick him up the . . .'

'Next case!' said the Chairman loudly.

Sebastian was led away.

The next time he was up in the same

9

position he had his pockets stuffed with money of all sorts and sizes.

'Fine me a hundred!' he bawled, chucking a handful of notes into the air. 'Two hundred! Three hundred! Go on! Fine me!' The policeman guarding the dock restrained him from throwing any more money about the Court. Already the public and some officials were knocking heads together in a common effort to pick up quickly.

When order was restored Sebastian Stanley was bound over to keep the peace for six months.

'Peace?' he shouted. 'What peace? Since I was born the world has been plagued with wars and rumours of wars driving us all into bankruptcy when the war was on, and quicker when it wasn't. Peace? I have never had any, so how the hell can I keep it?'

'It will be explained to you as you leave the Court,' said the Clerk, much affected. 'So kindly remove yourself and allow the business of the Court to proceed.'

'Hollyhocks,' said Sebastian, and did as requested.

All this rudeness created great interest in local newspaper editors, gently dozing in the public gallery, doubling up on reporting and wondering what to fill the paper with the following week. By next day the character of Sebastian Stanley was presented to the nation from the big papers under all kinds of humorous guises. It spread interest.

Philip saw it in three papers during the week and said to his mother, 'Is that one of ours?'

'*That*,' she said, 'is my bloody brother. He is a crook. Forget him.'

She died not long after, surviving her husband by eighteen years. During that eighteen years Philip, the only child, had married and divorced his wife. There had been no issue but bad feeling.

Philip was disturbed to find, after her death, that most of his mother's small estate had been spent on spoiling him. He was by profession a writer of precarious value, sometimes worth a bomb, sometimes not a light, as he wrote on his own blurb. A critics' darling he was an author most editors' and publishers' cashiers would hide from.

Once, when a fair cheque came to him his Bank Manager told him, 'Mr. Stanley, when you are in receipt of funds your first concern should be to your overdraft, the second to your neglected tax liabilities, the third to your living necessity and only the fourth to your pleasures, not in the opposite order.'

There followed a long period of inactivity on all Philip's fronts which even extended to refusing to open letters from the Bank, the Inland Revenue and Sundry Creditors. It was towards the end of this that he saw the report headed, 'Wealthy Recluse Causes Commotion in Court', upon reading which he asked the

11

question of his mother.

When his mother died almost his last monetary feed was turned off and it was then that he thought of his uncle. Being a writer of plots and reactions, he knew how useless would be the act of turning up at uncle's with hands outstretched in the long-lost nephew act. After much abortive thought he decided first to make a survey of the situation at Fairfield and put up at a small hotel in the town named in the press reports.

From there he ran his eye over the property, its situation, how the tradesmen called, what tradesmen called and what they brought. For this purpose he sat a lot on the common and at different times hired four different cars from different companies in order to park in the Avenue and see what happened at the front.

By March the fifteenth preceding the January murder, he had a fair picture of the set-up, its habits and its intakes, and so he left the town and went back to his mother's house, by that time, his, and sold her jewellery which provided a small but useful operational sum.

By that time he had almost daily deputations representing his Bank, the tax collector and other interested parties. He explained to them that things were not then settled but would soon be when things would be straightened.

It may seem incredible to some that these representatives, having been bamboozled for years, yet still had the faith in some obscure facet of human nature to go away and wait yet more.

Philip's game was then to make no attempt whatever to sell the property, and to lament to his creditors that people were constantly trying to buy and then after long delays, falling down on their promises and leaving the sale open again.

So nobody acted.

There was an uneasy feeling individually amongst the creditors that Philip's debts might be vast, and that any sudden legal action might leave a penny in the pound for each. Therefore each proceeded warily and with great compassion in the hope that their debt might be met even if all the others got sunk. As each one was doing this, the position was not exactly white one side and black the other, a fact which Philip played on with a skill born of long practice.

The true fact was that Philip's total debts were half the market value of the house, which was a necessary balance for his purpose.

He was at that time playing people for the benefit of his future.

The skilful manoeuvring continued with a visit to his ex-wife's husband (lover that was) with an urgent request for a loan. George, husband, paid over a couple of hundred so as not to have any more trouble with Philip, who had been trouble enough already.

13

Philip now made sure the wife heard of this, and made a second visit specially which resulted in 'Fight on Flat Balcony; Girl Knocks Ex-husband over into Fire Net: Near Murder, says Ex.'

Philip laughed all night.

Next day Philip made a call on a national daily newspaper office. He had written a lot of short stuff for them in the past and saw the Features Editor, Glenn Olsen.

'I have found a skeleton in the cupboard,' said Philip.

'Not another?' said Glenn.

'It seems I've got an outcast uncle who was some sort of big diddler in the war. It would make a story.'

'Well, don't try and flog it to us. We had enough libel over that little girl friend story of yours a few years back.'

'I had no idea she was a living person. I said so at the time—swore it on oath. Anyhow, I want to know about uncle for personal reasons. Are there any files going back that far?'

'Pop down and see Eddie Chapman. He'll fix you. But don't you send me anything about decimated uncles or in fact, any uncles at all.'

Eddie Chapman was earnest and beaverish. In three days, when Philip came to his office again, he had files on Sebastian Stanley dealing with the blacklisting in 1943 and also the troubles of 1918–20 and smaller items of

14

little consequence except one which was headed: 'Vanishing Gate-Crasher, Young Girl Disappears from Rich Man's Party'.

It was dated 1928 and followed by a few other paragraphs about it, growing smaller and shorter and finally fading out.

'Gillian Ward,' said Philip, making a note, and then looking up, 'I'm taking it down just to make sure I don't use it.'

'Oh yes!' said Eddie, and laughed. 'It makes a good rich uncle story, but if he lived like these said he did it's likely he's not rich now.'

'I understand he hasn't got a light now,' said Philip. 'Easy come, easy go, I expect. If you start life diddling then when you get old other people get quicker at diddling you. It's no good keeping up fencing at eighty.'

And he went back to mother's house by way of three pubs in Fleet Street, one in Poppins Court, two in the Strand, a call at the long bar in Waterloo Station and the bar on the train. Once home he laughed until he fell asleep.

It was unfortunate perhaps, that at that time he was working the whole thing as if it were some part of his novels, because in those tales, the baddie always walked out into the sunset unmolested, heading for his gold mine over the hill.

15

The meeting between uncle and nephew was unusual. Philip had waited in the drive knowing that Sebastian was going to get out his Rolls from the garage (once the coach-house) and drive to the Bank to draw his weekly cash to pay his tradesmen and housekeeper. It was part of the Big Sham designed to mislead the noseys.

Philip was surprised at the old man's tallness. He had imagined some kind of gnome, shrunken and bent from years of sitting protectively on his crock of gold. Instead he looked more like a retired undertaker's mute.

When the Rolls appeared and came down the drive, Philip stepped out from the bushes in front of it and held up his hand. Sebastian drove on. Philip, shivering within, held his ground. At the very last moment Sebastian braked and dug up gravel. The bumper was touching Philip's trouser legs.

'Get out of the bloody way,' said Sebastian, putting his head out of the window.

'I've got important news,' said Philip.

'You know what you can do with it.'

'Your sister is dead.'

'So is Queen Anne,' Sebastian shouted.

'I'm your nephew,' said Philip.

'I'm not buying any. Good day. Now get out of the way.'

'She told me certain things about you which might do you harm. I thought you ought to know what they are. I don't want the responsibility of having to know any old uncles. I'm keeping the decrepit side of my wife's family as it is.'

'Bloody hell!' said Sebastian and got out in a fury. 'Decrepit? Do you think I'm an impoverished old blood sucker like your wife's family?'

'How do you know what my wife's family are like? Don't judge people by yourself.'

Sebastian stared at Philip.

'You look like her,' he said. 'And you act like her. She was a bloody lunatic and obviously bred some more.'

He turned back to the car, then thought of something and looked back. 'You've said she's dead. What more is there?'

'There are people looking over the gate,' said Philip.

Sebastian looked past him, then bent and seized a border stone from the edge of the drive and threw it. The stone crashed against the gatepost, but by then the watchers had fled.

'My mother was a better shot than that,' said Philip, contemptuously. 'But then she said you weren't any good at anything. Anyhow, that mob heard what you were shouting and I don't want them to confuse me with a bawling old idiot, so goodbye.'

17

'I've already said it,' said Sebastian. 'And walk fast or I'll mow you down.'

Philip started walking, then started to run, then dived off the drive into a bush. The car dug up gravel again as it stopped.

'Just a minute,' Sebastian called. 'What did you come for?'

Philip pulled himself out of the bushes and started picking leaves and broken twigs off his suit.

'She said you needed money,' he said, busy at his cleaning. 'She said you were always writing to her for money and she wanted me to see you if anything happened to her.'

By this time they were almost out on the road and people were walking by and Sebastian thought it was possible some had stopped walking by and were hiding behind the wall beside the gatepost, listening.

'What proof have you got you're her son?' said Sebastian.

Philip brought a gold locket from his pocket, opened it and showed the old man the picture of his mother.

'That's her,' said Sebastian. 'But you could have stolen it.'

'And then come here and show it to you, knowing you're hard up and likely to try and claim—?'

'Come to the house,' said Sebastian, reversing sharply up the drive. 'We can't talk here!'

CHAPTER TWO

1

Philip Stanley was tuned for rapid appreciation as he entered the hall after Sebastian. It was wide, very wide, with arched openings halfway down. From inside those two staircases rose up. The hall ran from front to back of the big house, and at the end was an arched opening with a set of stained glass windows within.

A carpet covered the hall floor, and there were carpets on each staircase. Good carpets, thick carpets, but not so clean as one might have expected. The paint on the walls and big, wide doors within the arches was faded, but looked as if it needed washing more than repainting.

There were brass pots around with ferns, aspidistra, and palms flanking the stained glass window niche. It was all rich, yet faded like a powdered, wrinkled dowager.

But rich. That was what Philip was quick to see. That was what he had come to see.

'Come in here,' said Sebastian opening a door on the left.

They went into a great room with high windows looking out to the front. There were six armchairs and two sofas, big as elephants, all in buttoned leather; bookcases, more carpets and a stale smell of cigars and dust as if the windows had not been opened for some time.

There was a big polished table behind the sofa before the stone fireplace, and carrying three bottles of Scotch, some tumblers and a soda siphon on a silver tray. These items were the only ones that did not seem to have that odd dullness coming from lack of care, or use.

Philip could even see Sebastian's favourite chair by the shine of its leather against the frosty look of the others.

'Have a drink,' said Sebastian, pouring some for both.

'Yes,' said Philip, looking round at the books, the cabinets, a walnut grand piano over in a corner by the end window, paintings hanging on walls papered, it seemed, with velvet, and last of all, a safe crouching by the side of the fireplace like some green and brass lion.

And the brass of the handles and dial were bright and clean. Their brightness reflected in Philip's eyes. Sebastian poured generously.

'Weren't you going out?' said Philip.

'No,' said Sebastian. 'Here. Swallow.'

'I'll have some soda,' said Philip.

'Pansy,' said Sebastian and walked away to the grand piano by which he stood and gazed out of the window. 'She's dead then.'

'Yes.'

Sebastian turned back and stared hard at Philip. 'What do you do?' he said.

'Write.'

'You mean you've been sponging on your mother all your life?'

'Not quite all. I make some money now and then.'

'What did she leave?'

'Not sorted out yet.'

'She always had a bit of her own. Your father was a saving sort of man, I hear. Never met him. Haven't seen her since before you were born. She had her own house, didn't she?'

'Oh yes. I might be lucky, when it's all sorted out. But I had to see you. It was her wish.'

'When did she wish it?' Sebastian was suspicious.

'Not long ago. When she felt she was going to die.'

'Drink up,' said Sebastian going back to the drink tray. 'This isn't Alcoholics Anonymous.' He poured more. 'What do you write?'

'Novels. That sort of thing.'

'Why did she want you to see me?'

'She had this idea you were hard up. Business trouble. Said you were too much of a gambler ever to do any good.'

'Did she? Silly bitch.' He walked back to the piano. 'Well, she wasn't a gambler. Always wanted security. Funny idea that. There isn't

21

any. Just a word. Now what the hell did she think she could do for me anyway?'

'I've told you. She thought you might need help, and I was to give you some if you did need it. Anyone with a spark of decency would have been grateful.'

'No one ever accused me of decency,' said Sebastian. 'Certainly not your mother. Depraved was her word, I recall. Curious woman. I borrowed some money off her once when I was starting up in business. I did all right, but she kept making such a fuss about getting her money back that I just wouldn't pay it. One gets like that when people start nagging. Drink up. This isn't the Band of Hope.'

He went back to the table. Philip drank up. He did not want to get drunk at that particular time, but it was necessary to keep in step with his Uncle. That was part of the game that had to be played right through.

And from the way Sebastian was mopping it up, the game seemed just what Philip had been looking for. In fact it was an unexpected gilding of the whole nebulous scene. The sun was coming out on his horizon.

He took another drink.

'You've got some nice stuff here,' he said. 'I suppose you'd flog it if you needed to.' He crossed the room to the fireplace and looked at the picture above it. 'What's that? A Constable?'

'A copy,' said Sebastian quickly and turned away.

'Hm. I like the old safe. What's it run on—acetylene?'

'It's safe. That's all that matters, not age.'

Philip saw, what was not obvious at first, that the back—the weakest part, was actually built into the wall.

Sebastian started talking about his heroic efforts to supply the fighting men of two world wars. He became most impressive, dramatic even as the Scotch spoke with more and more feeling.

Philip was beginning to feel the overheating effects of the drink in his brain. He would have liked to stop off there, but Sebastian went on and on until Philip began to fear his returning to the table and threatening with the raised bottle.

At some time after three—Philip heard a clock chiming something somewhere and thought it was about three strokes, but could not be sure—relief came.

Sebastian threw his tumbler into the fireplace when about to pour yet more, then collapsed face down on the table.

Philip helped him right on to the polished surface, turned him on his back, crossed his arms on his chest, then looked round, took an aspidistra from a pot and stuck it in the nerveless hands. Then he fell over.

He crawled about for some time, like some

23

shabby tiger lost in a leather jungle and finally climbed up a chair, like a mountaineer battling for the summit, and stood swaying, holding chair with one hand and head with the other.

He felt sure his head was falling off the way it was swinging round like a bucket on a string.

'Good God!' he muttered. 'Water. Water!'

He made a long, curving track to the door and just got the handle before he fell over. He hit his forehead on the panels and the shock jangled his brain inside his skull as if the whole mass had come loose.

He got out into the hall and went wandering through the slowly moving scene, swerving, clutching at things for support.

'My God, I'm bad!' he shouted at one point. 'I'm ill!'

By some means and after opening many doors and almost falling through them, he reached the kitchen, a large room with the usual appointments and a great porcelain sink. He clawed his way to it and clung to its edge for a while, watching the window behind it climb up the wall so far then come down and start up again. He reached a tap and turned it on, then bent and put his head under the stream. It was dead cold. The shock went right down his spine but it seemed to shake the brain back on to a recognisable track.

He stayed there a minute or more, then straightened, water coming off his hair and face and dripping over his jacket.

It was then the woman walked in from somewhere. She came into his blurred scene from the right and stopped in front of him.

She was about thirty, fairly tall and with a fine, generous figure, black hair, a perfect complexion and bright blue eyes. He saw all this like an impressionist painting through water-filled lashes.

'My God,' he said vaguely. 'Sexy!'

'You're tight,' the woman said. She took a towel from behind an open door and threw it so it wrapped round his drenched head.

He mumbled some thanks and started to rub, swaying a bit. She went and got hold of his arm, steadying him and at the same time, feeling his biceps.

'You seem strong,' she said, holding on. He uncovered his face.

'Physical strength,' he said, not too clearly. 'No moral stamina. Weak.'

She punched him in the chest and he went back against the sink.

'What's tha—' he said and grunted into a gasp.

'I'm putting in some stamina,' she said and smacked his face hard, twice. ' 'Tis the only way for drunks. There! Now sit down.' She pulled him to the table and shoved him down into a chair. Then she got a fistful of his wet hair and pulled his head up to look at her. 'Where's he?'

He waved his hand and hit it on the table

edge. 'There,' he said, waving in a wide arc.

'You be seated there,' she said. 'In a moment you'll be better. You must be a favoured client, I'm thinking.'

'I'm—his uncle,' Philip said, and felt his face where she had smacked it. 'That is—vice versa, so forth—'

'You wait there.' She went out through the hall and into the big room where Sebastian lay in state on the table. The woman stared a moment then stood back and burst into a peal of laughter that looked as if it might burst her tight trouser suit.

The sound opened Sebastian's eyes, and she went up to the table and took the plant from his hands.

'Come on,' she said. 'Get up. I'm holding the room still for you.'

She hauled him off the table, made him stand, undid his collar then walked him on his rubber knees out of the room, into the hall and up the left hand stairs. At the top he tried to hang on to the landing rail.

'Important nephew,' he growled. 'Portant.'

'Come on,' she said thinly.

She opened a door, took him into a large bedroom and shoved him on to a four-poster bed. At this point he got his arm round her neck and tried to pull her down on top of him, muttering passionately.

'You'll be lucky,' she said taking his arm away and straightening. 'You just sleep that lot

26

off. I'll call you for supper.'

'Love me, Med!' he said, looking at the ceiling with some pain screwing his eyes up.

She went out and slammed the door. Then, singing a verse of *The Mountains of Mourne* with some improper variations she went back to the kitchen.

Philip had pulled himself together a good deal and looked almost steady.

'I didn't know he had any women here,' he said, watching her with an awakening of his normal appreciation.

'He hasn't,' she said. 'My name is Med Cusack. I'm the housekeeper.'

'What's Med stand for? I've never heard it before.'

'Medina. I'm named after the river me father was drownin' in the day I was born. He was the captain of a ship. As you can tell from my illegitimate speech I am Irish and I come from Glasgow where I was born. 'Tis a bit confusin', like the old Chinese Rabbi from Prague, whose descent was exceedingly vague—No, I'd best not go on. You'll be noticin' I'm making some tea or would you sooner some coffee for your head? 'Tis not a bad head to look at. I had a handsome husband myself once. Big strong feller you'd have thought he would be at it all times, but he preferred looking at the girls on the telly. He drove into a bus lookin' at some girl's sweater on the pavement. That's how I'm a widow. My

27

sister said I'm like the song, a Tit Widow. You'd think he'd have seen the bus, though. Shaun his name was. You don't want to marry an Irishman. 'Tis all talk and talk and very beautiful it is, no doubt, in certain moods for sure it's very beautiful, but they do say the more a dog barks the less energy he's got for bitin'.

'My sister Lorna, now, she married a small little feller almost without any tongue at all you might say and she's laughin' all the time even though he doesn't seem to say anythin', but you've got to watch it when she isn't there, too. Would you like sugar, now?'

'No thanks.' He got up. 'What do you do here then?'

'I clean just certain rooms. It's too big. I'd need all my sisters and a few more to keep all this place clean, so I make the rule, just so much, no more.

'He only eats once in a day, you see, that is in the evenin', and he has a good fill up then which keeps him stoked up till the next night. 'Tis not much trouble.'

'You live here then?'

'Oh no. I live with my sister Eileen. Her husband's on the gravel.'

'On the gravel?'

'He drives a truck full of little stones they fill him up with at the gravel pit. Funny sort of man. He should have married a footballer—a lady one of course, for he's always talkin' of

28

nothing else. I suppose he'd even get excited if he knew Eileen was havin' a bit of fun with a footballer from the town team, which you can't blame her.'

'When do you come here?'

'I come a couple of hours in the mornin', and then does shoppin' if anythin's wanted which it usually is, then come back the afternoon and go after cleanin' up supper and then he gets drunk again till next day.'

'What does he do now?'

She laughed.

'I don't know what he does. He don't seem to do nothin' much, but then he's a man of secrets. It's all secrets. You go to clean some place unexpected and he shouts out "Not there! Not there!" and that kind of thing. I've got used to it. Is the tea too strong for you?'

'I'll be honest. I can't taste anything yet.'

'Funny he's seein' you like that,' she said. 'He don't normally let anybody in. Only women. He'll let women in. Always women. You might say he yearns for women. P'raps he was bottle fed. They say bottle fed babies yearn for mothers later on. Like my husband. He didn't really want a wife, just a mother. But I don't really know with your uncle, though, I don't.'

'Do you like him?' Philip said.

She stared then and began to smile.

'There's a question!' she said and laughed. 'Yes, I like him, though he's a wicked old

29

bastard and everybody knows it. But he's a rebel. He stands for himself. That's what I like in a man. You're married I should say.'

'Divorced.'

'My sister Les is divorced. They both got married again and then went back together so the other two want to divorce them. They're crazy, that lot. Will you go back to her?'

'Only to cut her throat.'

She laughed with him.

'Well, 'tis honest, any rate.'

Sebastian came in looking like the ghost of Banquo just dragged out of a ditch.

'He's going to stay. Get a room ready,' he said.

'Stayin' is he? Well, that'll be more work so I'd best stay as well. I'll get me things. And one or two other things if he's staying. Food, like.'

She went out. They heard a small car start and draw away. Sebastian grinned like a vulture.

'They all think she's my personal tart,' he said. 'It's very comforting—their thoughts.'

'She is a very attractive woman,' said Philip. 'But I've no doubt she looks after herself. She and all her sisters.'

'She's been selling the product?' said Sebastian, opening the kitchen table drawer and taking a cigar out. 'She paints a good picture. Only her father wasn't the Irish captain of the *Queen Mary* in her heyday. He was a brewer's bargee, with a crew of one,

30

running beer from the Isle of Wight to the mainland. On the day she was born he wasn't drowning in the Medina, but was so drunk in a Newport pub that he thought he was.'

'We all tell a lot of lies,' said Philip, watching his uncle light his cigar with a lighter attached to a gas cooker. 'And you know that'll spoil the cigar—if the cigar is worth spoiling, of course.'

'You have that wrong, haven't you boy?' said Sebastian grinning again. 'The cigar is worth not spoiling, but I have not the taste to be able to tell a good one from a fine one, or vintage from non-vintage, so you can stuff that where the monkey put the nuts.'

He regarded his nephew with half closed eyes and smoked very thoughtfully.

'I don't think you came to see if I needed money,' he said, carefully. 'I think you want money. I think you came here to get some out of me, and I'm going to keep you here until you admit that's what you came for.'

Sebastian got an unexpected reaction.

'That suits me,' said Philip, and then, seeing the brief look of puzzlement pass over Sebastian's face he added, 'so long as Medina Cusack stays.'

Sebastian straightened up and looked more relaxed.

'You'll find her a hard task, me boy,' he said, looking at the burning end of his cigar. 'But please yourself.'

That wasn't the reaction Philip had expected. The game was becoming interesting for Philip. Like chess, but with somebody dead at the end.

3

A bell rang. Carefully, Sebastian put his cigar down on the edge of the kitchen table, watched Philip a moment, then turned and went out somewhere to the back of the house. A door was opened with a bang as if Sebastian had crashed it against a wall.

'Misses ordered this lot just now,' a voice said. 'Thought I'd bring it right away. Going home, see?'

'What is it?' said Sebastian.

'Well, I'm the butcher aren't I? It ain't milk. Shall I bring it in?'

'Just put it on the floor.'

'I usually bring it in. I want the tray, see?'

'I'll send it back.'

'But I want it.'

'I said I'll send it back, now beggar off. Put it down and beggar off!'

'You look here. I want my tray. Usually I puts it on the table in there and takes—'

'Get out of it will you? Give me that and go!' There was a pause.

'You're bonkers,' the butcher said. 'You want to watch you don't wake up one morning with your bloody throat cut. I'll not leave the tray. I want it for tonight. Go and get a dish or something or go without the bloody lot.'

'Tip the meat on the shelf there.'

'It's dirty there.'

'The meat's wrapped, isn't it?'

'Only paper. Gone through now with the blood. Still. It's up to you. You want to eat dust, you sodden well eat dust. It's no skin off my nose.'

Philip listened enthralled. The cigar began to char the table edge. At last Sebastian came back, after slamming the back door.

'I don't know where they get 'em from!' he said.

'You forgot your cigar.'

Sebastian picked it up and resumed smoking. Then he threw it in the sink.

'You need calm for smoking cigars,' he cried. 'Calm!' He sat on the edge of the table. 'Tell me about your mother. Did she push you? She was always trying to get her own way. Used to blackmail father with hysterics and threatening to jump off the roof.'

'Sometimes she used to push it. I wasn't so sure about Jennifer myself, but she was. That's how it happened.'

'Who's Jennifer?'

'My ex-wife.'

'She made you marry?'

'No. It was all above board. In white and a flat belly. It was just that Mother thought she was right for me. Women get like that. I don't know why. I don't think it's because they like the other woman, but just that they think it will solve something for you. Or them.'

'What about your father? He the same? I never met him.'

'No. He rather used to give in, but as I got older I saw he wasn't giving in, but just doing what suited him. He used to work a lot. Bring it home. Stay late at the office.'

'There was some gas about a divorce then. My friends told me. About twenty years back.'

'There was some gas, as you say. In fact it would have been more, but they didn't want to spoil my career. I was at Dulwich then. A very good school. The sacrifice didn't pay off. I was sacked the next year.'

'This divorce was your mother?'

'Oh no. It was Daddy and his late nights at the office. He didn't say whose office. He said it was because he couldn't sleep. Do you sleep well?'

Sebastian stared sharply.

'Well enough.'

'They say the older you get the lighter it gets. Sleep.'

'I do well enough.'

Medina came back.

'What in the devil's name's that bleedin' all over the passage out there? Get a dish, take that sodden paper off it and stack it proper.'

With a pathological interest, Philip watched

his uncle go out of the room and do as he was told.

'You've heard of this cuttin' off nose to spite face,' she said. 'Well, there he is personally. Another row with the man, I suppose. I wonder anybody comes here at all.'

'Does he always quarrel with them?'

'You'd think sometimes there was going to be murder. He rubs 'em up wrong. I reckon if there's anybody could start a fight with the Salvation Army 'twould be him.'

She went to a cupboard and took out a lot of cleaning things and a broom.

'I'll go do that room for you,' she said.

She went out. Philip heard Sebastian slamming about somewhere at the back of the house.

You'd think sometimes there was going to be murder, thought Philip. But no, but no, but no. It looks too easy. Too much a gift. There's a lot to be settled.

CHAPTER THREE

1

Though murder was the theme of Philip's long and careful planning, the fact that he was now right in the scene of the coming death frightened him. Though it was still coming, all

35

right, he would sooner keep his back to it until the moment came when he had to turn and fire.

Murder was not something that he wished to soak in for reasons of pure excitement, or experience. It was an unpleasant means to a pleasant end.

He sat at the vast scrubbed kitchen table watching Med with a pleasurable lust.

'Does he have any friends at all?' he said.

'There's some calls,' she said, peeling potatoes. 'It's business I'd say to judge by the shoutin' and bangin' that goes on in there.'

'I didn't think he did any business now.' Philip was puzzled as to what the callers came for. Weeks ago he had watched visitors come and go, but most had seemed to be tradesmen at the back door. Those at the front had been few and far between and had seemed for the main, door-to-door men.

'There's lots of mail,' she said. 'Always scribblin' away at letters all the time. "Take these to the postbox, Med" he says, mostly every day if not more. My husband never wrote any letters but he got a few and I didn't know for what they were till after he was gone and the men came and took the car and the fridge and all that. It seems that was what the letters was about.'

'And that's what he does all day? Write letters and see these people who call?'

'It varies about them comin',' she said.

'Sometimes there'll be nobody for a week, other times there's a half dozen in a couple of days. You can't tell, but I'm thinkin' he knows what to expect, for he never has me to let them in.'

Philip felt a warm glow momentarily overcoming his lust as he realised that the whole scene was becoming easier, simpler, almost made for him. He had been ready to make any adjustments to his plan after he had got into the house and seen how things were, but the layout now made it almost unnecessary.

In fact it was almost as if it had never been necessary to do any previous thinking at all.

'Where is he now?' Philip said.

'Dozin',' she said. 'Always now till dinner, in his chair in the study there. He gets so tired you'd wonder if he gets any sleep of nights sometimes.'

'Do you often stay overnight?'

'Now and again, but not often. When I do it's hard for me to get any sleep for he's always hollerin' and bangin' at my door about somethin' or the other and I know what the other is so I don't answer. So now it's if anybody stays.'

'To make work easier?'

'You'd never guess. He has the thinkin' of a lunatic man, for he fears someone stayin' here might do him in, so he tells me.'

Philip felt a sharp stab of uneasiness.

'Why?'

'Seems he thought somebody tried once, but you can never tell, for he's a cunnin' old devil, and I'm not jokin' there, for he's like a kid tryin' to get round you, but in the end you know what he's after. He makes things up to try and get on my soft side, and if I let that happen I'd be a loser. But I couldn't anyway. He gives me the creepies, snaky old bastard. In that way, sexy, I mean. I like him because he's a wicked old devil and makes me laugh with his cunnin' ways, but him touchin' me—' She grimaced.

'There used to be big parties here. I've seen some of the old newspapers.'

'I'll bet he was an old ram,' she said. 'There are women call sometimes. There's always a lot of laughin' and goin' on, but sometimes I've seen them go flamin' out in a wild temper so you can guess what you want.' She filled a saucepan with water.

'There was a feller once I let in by accident and I heard him shoutin' about how the old devil had insulted his wife and there was some shoutin' and "If you was younger I'd you-know-what" sort of talk. You know,' she became thoughtful, 'sometimes I think he asks for trouble meanin' to get some.'

Better and better, mused Philip. Better and better and better still.

'That's what happened with my wife,' he said. 'Only she liked being insulted.'

38

She looked at him keenly.

'Like so, indeed?' she said.

'There was a divorce and so on. She married him.'

'Ah.' Her interest seemed to fade. 'I must get in with this dinner. It has to be half past seven.' She turned away to a cupboard.

'Just one thing,' he said, getting up, 'do there have to be any more drunk sessions? I'm not sure I can stand it. Not like today.'

'There'll be no more tonight,' she said. 'After a bash he's teetotal, militant against it. He's crazy as a coot. You'll learn.'

Philip went out and wandered through the hall. Now and again he opened doors and looked into the rooms. The furniture was sheeted, and the sheets grey with dust. Cobwebs decorated the ornate ceiling plasters, mirrors were almost opaque brown and the gilt a greenish yellow. Daylight from the windows was filtered with dust, dirt and webs and there was everywhere the warm, dusty smell of a comfortable decay.

Philip looked particularly for pictures and valuable ornaments, but there was nothing standing or hanging which he thought could be worth more than a few pounds.

The rooms themselves would have made excellent sets for films of luxurious life, except that Philip had been told natural cobwebs did not photograph as well as the spray-on sort.

He halted at the study door and listened.

He could hear faint snoring, but to make sure he opened the door and looked in.

Sebastian was practically unconscious in the one polished leather chair, head drooping.

Philip shut the door and again turned to the stairs. He started as he saw Med standing just past the foot of one flight, watching him.

'You'll want to see your room properly,' she said. ' 'Tis up this side.'

She started up the stairs and Philip followed. At the top she stopped and turned to him.

'He's still off, then?' she said.

'Dead off,' he said.

'My father was a sea captain,' she said, going on again. 'We were used to him dropping off just when and where he felt like it. 'Twas nothin' unusual.'

She opened a door, one removed from the door which faced the staircase. They walked into a bedroom which overlooked the front gardens with three tall windows.

'A four poster,' said Philip.

' 'Tis a modern mattress, though,' she said and sat and bounced on it. ' 'Tis all that comfortable for sure.'

Philip looked round. It was a good room, very Victorian, except for the bed, and very comfortable, including the bed, she said.

Med remained sitting on it, watching him as he went to the fireplace and picked a carriage clock off the mantel.

'What did you come for?' she said.

He looked round at her.

'I came to make the acquaintance of my uncle. My mother died recently, and Sebastian was her brother. She seemed to think he might need money, but by the look of things I don't think he does.'

'He wants nothin',' she said. 'Not in the money way. What made you think he might, then?'

'Don't be so damned suspicious,' he said. 'I didn't think he might; my mother did.'

'How can I help bein' suspicious that anyone would want to help Sebastian Stanley, except to help him out of this world?'

'You know what happens if you kill somebody. You get nicked.'

'I don't know that could be right,' she said, eyeing him levelly. 'I'm friendly with a man and he says there's more murders done than anybody ever finds out about.'

'It isn't worth risking you'll do one nobody's going to know about.'

'All life is risks, like gettin' married. My mother used to say if you venture nothin' you get fanny all.'

He put the clock back, turned and leant against the mantel shelf.

'This is funny sort of talk,' he said.

'It was you made me think of it,' she said.

A chill held him still, his muscles freezing. He waited till the rigor passed, then said, 'Now

41

how in hell could I have done that?'

'I like to look at a man and guess whether he's got the guts to do certain things. It's a game of mine.' They watched each other.

'I know,' he said, grinning. 'It was Sebastian who gave you this idea, with his fear of everyone wanting to do him in.'

She shook her head slowly and smiled.

'No, no. 'Tis my game, I tell you. I guess what a man's got in him and then find out for myself, right or wrong.'

'And you guess I'm a killer?' he said, going towards her.

'No. I guess what you *could* be. That's different.'

'It's not very complimentary,' he said.

She got up and turned to the door.

'I must get on with that bloody cookin',' she said. She went out and closed the door behind her.

He sat on the bed and thought that perhaps things did not look as good as they had. The ruddy woman was fey. She could see inside.

And then branching off, he wondered if she might know where the crock of gold was hidden in that house.

2

'Steak!' shouted Sebastian in sudden fury. 'You know I can't eat steak! In thirty years I've

42

never had a set of teeth that could sit still eating steak! You did it on purpose! You wanted to make me mad! You stupid great Irish clodhopping cosy! Steak, my God!'

'Oh, suck it, then,' said Med. 'It's for your guest, your nephew. I beat it well. A baby could eat that with his gums, now. You have a go.'

Sebastian stood up, threw down his napkin and pointed into her face.

My heavens, *East Lynne*, thought Philip.

'You did it on purpose you—you wench,' said Sebastian, shaking. 'Steak! You know what I think about steak! What guest? Since when did my guests matter more than me? Steak!'

'Sit your bottom and get stuck in,' she said angrily. 'You can eat it and stop the fussin'.' She marched out.

Philip watched the movement of her back appreciatively and imagined its actuation in other situations. She did not slam the door. It was the second time he had noticed she had a very soft way with doors.

'She's a bitch,' said Sebastian. 'She did it deliberately to steam me up. Steak and French fried—'

'The culinary French for French fried is chips,' said Philip, shortly. 'Now sit down and behave yourself like an adult. Why on earth should the woman steam you up? Don't imagine things.'

43

Sebastian craned his head over the table. He looked like an unamiable vulture.

'By the lord, you talk just like she did! Sermons and Criticisms and Good Talk and crap, day in, day out. How in hell do sisters come like that when they come from the same stock?'

Philip started to eat, ignoring Sebastian. Sebastian walked about the room for a minute or two, then sat down and started eating. It was true his teeth objected, for there was a continuous plastic clicking which seemed to be magnified by his voice box so that Philip thought he might swallow the set instead of the steak.

'Are you fussy?' said Sebastian, swallowing so that his apple slid up and down a foot. Philip imagined an ostrich swallowing a cricket ball, and then found he had difficulty in swallowing himself.

At any rate, he thought, after hearing Sebastian's teeth eating steak, disposal could only be a good thing for the old man. He wanted to chuckle and then felt sick.

'Fussy as hell,' he replied, half choking. 'Your woman cooks well.'

'Why don't you call her Med?' said Sebastian, sharply. 'Want to hide your want of her body? Never like a Stanley to have a false shyness. Unless you're trying to fool me into thinking you haven't felt anything.'

Despite teeth handicaps, he ate like a

deprived shark and finished before Philip.

'I think you have a filthy mind,' said Philip, pushing his plate away.

'There are only two sorts of people,' said Sebastian. 'Those who have filthy minds and those who pretend they haven't. Why waste energy kidding yourself? You never kid anybody else.'

'Did anyone ever suggest you ought to drown yourself?' said Philip, pleasantly.

'Ring the bell,' said Sebastian. 'Drown. Used to give big parties here. There's a big conservatory off the drawing room. Huge. Palms and God knows. Used to have a gardener just for inside there. There's a lily pond in the middle. Used to grow exotics in there as well. In the water.

'I had a row one night and the man shoved me face down in the pond and tried to hold me there. Meant to finish me, that fellow. More than forty years ago now. He's dead.'

Philip rang a bell by the door and came back to the table.

'How did you survive?' he said.

'A girl came in behind him. She crowned him with a big pot. It burst all over the place, mould everywhere. Then she pulled me out. By then, the man was dead.'

'Dead?' said Philip, startled.

'Shut up,' said Sebastian.

Med came in. Philip made a note that the old man's hearing was good. At least he could

45

hear when people were coming, if he wanted to.

'So you ate it,' said Med, taking up the plates. 'Old bag of wind.' She went out again.

'Nobody saw, you see,' said Sebastian. 'Just this girl and me. Well, I got him by the ankles and towed him out into the garden. It was dark and I left him under a bush. He's still right near there now. Not much left, I suppose.'

'Nobody asked about him?'

'He was having trouble. His wife thought he had run off with somebody. Nobody seemed to ask. It was very lucky, all round. But then I found the girl shouldn't have been there anyway. She crashed the party. It's surprising how things fall out sometimes. Very surprising.'

'And you kept it hidden for the sake of somebody you didn't even know?'

'I never care for publicity in private affairs,' said Sebastian, taking cheese. 'It is a very dangerous habit to get into, letting everybody know your weaknesses.'

'Did you pay the girl?' said Philip, eating biscuits.

'It was ironic,' said Sebastian, reminiscently. 'Nobody asked after the man, who was murdered, but everybody asked about the girl, who shouldn't have been there.'

'Why?' said Philip, with keenly innocent interest. 'Did she disappear too?'

'She feared Nemesis in a bowler hat at the

back door,' said Sebastian. 'And insisted on hiding in the house till it all died down. It was a most confusing situation, as I was at the time having a sort of lit-a-deux with Lady Grafitti or some such. I forget her name now. She was a most excitable girl, given to sudden giggles and writing extremely rude words on brick walls. Always brick walls. I suppose bricks roused her sexual imagination. I'm afraid little else did. Of all the girls I shared confidences with she was the most like a cold Yorkshire pudding.

'But she was excessively jealous, and it was a matter of continuous alarm to me that the girls would meet on the landing somewhere. However, in the end, she went.'

'Which? I'm confused.'

'Her ladyship went because her husband came and tried to sell her to me, without knowing that for me, there was nothing left to buy, and cold Yorkshire pudding is not my rave, as they say.'

Philip sat back and took a long thin cigar from a packet in his pocket.

'You fascinate me,' he said. 'But I should have thought that with your egotistical religion you would have had no trouble in getting rid of cold pud, of whatever breed.'

'I have explained to you that her idea of sex excitement was to rush up and write it on a wall,' said Sebastian. 'I should have been suspicious at the beginning, but in the course of my siege I rather ignored it and then found

47

that the police were looking for a couple who were publishing obscenities, and, of all things, I let that become a little noose for my ankle.'

'It's all very discreditable,' said Philip, making copious mental notes, 'but why did you hide the body to help someone you didn't know?'

'She saved me from drowning,' said Sebastian, taking a cigar from a box which he had kept to his side of the table. 'They were wild days in the twenties. People today don't realise the extent to which the improper flourished then. All the drugs, sex, drink, perversion that we hear of today is a reprise of what happened in the twenties. I suppose life goes like a tide. Coming in and up to the cast-away cigarette packets and the discarded contraceptives on the beach and then withdrawing for a period to the cleanliness of the sea, and then coming back on a due tide to contact more excreta.'

'Leave out the philosophy,' said Philip, with unusual patience. 'Why did you help a girl who was a stranger when you laid yourself open to being an accomplice?'

Sebastian took his time. He lit his cigar, then carefully laid it down on top of the cheese dish and looked at Philip.

'When one has had a while of living with a giggling pudding with hands full of chalk and finds one's life saved by a girl full of new promise and beauty, the reaction can be an

48

immense tide of sheer determination to get it at all costs.'

'Yes, I can see that,' said Philip, slowly. He watched Sebastian pick up his cigar again. 'Why did the man try and drown you at the beginning? Was that about a woman, too?'

'There was some complicated involvement with his fiancée, some money he owed, some side issue of his brother's wife, or his sister, was it? Perhaps both. I don't remember now.'

'You seem to have lived like a Louis of Versailles.'

'I had a bloody good time,' said Sebastian. 'I regret it ever ended. It kept one awake, alert, watchful.'

'Yes, I can understand that,' said Philip, very thoughtfully.

He was thoughtful because for some reason that he could not place just then, he had the feeling that things were not going to be as easy as they had appeared an hour or two ago.

The life of Sebastian Stanley gave him the impression that his uncle had been tutored into the splendid evil of the human mind to a far wider extent than Philip had. He felt almost a child by comparison.

But of course, he thought, relaxing, it could all be a fat volume of lies.

But, he recalled, tightening again, there were those old news cuttings.

'Just as a matter of interest,' said Philip, 'did you ever help anybody quite selflessly?'

49

'I was forever doing it,' said Sebastian. 'I could tell at a moment when a fellow's wife was unworthy of him, so I quite often helped a little. There were many times when—'

'What did you do with that body?'

'I was at the time a very strong and virile young man,' said Sebastian. 'I got a shovel and buried him.'

'And he's still out there now, under your window?'

'I sincerely hope so. That is why, despite my fear of thieves and burglars, I have never had a dog. They dig up bones, you know.'

'I could blackmail you,' said Philip, reflectively.

'I doubt it,' said Sebastian. 'You would find in-superable obstacles.'

'What did happen about the girl?'

'In the end the gate-crashing story was regarded as a rumour. There was no proof she had ever been here at all, and so it all faded away.'

'What was her name?' said Philip, casually.

'I don't remember now,' said Sebastian. 'It's all a very long time ago. I was thirty then, you see. A very long time ago.'

'What sort of business were you in then?'

'Buying and selling. Anything. Ships or sealing wax. So long as I bought low and sold high it suited me. I never saw any of the stuff I bought. Arms was a good sideline. There were so many lying around after the first war and

50

what we now call developing countries were clamouring for that kind of sophisticated Western further education. It all worked out very well until the slump came. Yes.' Sebastian looked thoughtful. 'Very well indeed.'

'Do you do anything now?'

Sebastian carefully removed ash from his cigar on the top of the cheese.

'I am very old,' he said. 'One is not so steady. The nerves get looser, you know. In business one has to be alert and courageous. One mustn't be frightened. Are you often frightened?'

'Frightened? That's a curious question. Do you mean frightened more or less than average? If so, how do you measure it?'

'Supposing, for example,' said Sebastian, 'somebody offered you a large sum of money to commit murder. Would you have the courage to do it, or would you be too frightened?'

'I think you're off your head,' said Philip, grinding his cigar out in an ashtray.

'It is not an unknown proposition,' said Sebastian. 'In fact, since no one hangs any more, I believe it gets more popular every day.'

Philip felt very uneasy. This was the second time in three hours that murder had been suggested, and with his conscience bad, the force of evil bit him harder than it would have an innocent man.

Sebastian watched him and then began to

51

laugh. 'You don't care for my sense of humour?' he said.

'Your woman said you had an obsession about visitors killing you,' said Philip. 'I suppose this is a facet of it.'

A bell rang in the room. Sebastian was galvanised like a dead frog's leg. He got up, went to the door and out, slamming it after him.

Philip got up and went to the door to listen. That the front door bell sounded inside the study was unusual but interesting. It made almost sure that Med didn't hear it, and Sebastian's instant response made almost sure that if anybody else did hear it, he would get to the door first.

Philip listened. There were voices out in the hall, but the door was too thick to let him hear words. His hand hovered on the handle, then drew back. Instinctively, he went back to the table and sat down.

Sebastian came in with a short man following. The visitor was about five feet high and as broad. Fat, he waddled, rolling from foot to foot as he came. His face was fat, grinning slyly under a bottle nose. His eyes were a penetrating blue in lids wrinkled with constant, humourless grinning.

'This is John Ball,' said Sebastian. 'Pimp, ponce, prostitute's bully and rough-houser for rent.'

And Ball grinned wider, as if pleased with his qualification.

CHAPTER FOUR

1

Sebastian went over to his favourite armchair and sat down. John Ball followed, head almost hanging, hat in his hands, then stopped and stood in front of the seated man.

Sebastian let him stand, as he let Philip go on sitting at the table by himself.

'You can ignore my nephew over there,' said Sebastian. 'He's learning the business.'

Philip did not trouble to look askance, but shrugged slightly and watched the fat, subservient doughnut man standing awaiting orders.

'Well,' said Sebastian. 'Get on with it.'

'I have spoken to Mr. Gleeson—' began Ball.

'Naturally you've spoken to Mr. Gleeson,' Sebastian cut in. 'That's what I told you to do. Get on with it.'

'He wants fifteen thousand,' said Ball.

'You jest, you pouf,' laughed Sebastian.

'That's what he said.' Ball fumbled his hat round and round by the brim, revolutions increasing with the tension of his nerves.

'Does he think I have started a welfare society?' said Sebastian. 'Ten.'

'Oh I'm afraid he wouldn't. Not ten,' said

Ball, nervously. 'No, not ten. Fifteen. He was very definite.'

'He's off his onion,' said Sebastian pleasantly. 'Ten.'

The hat turned faster.

'He might take fourteen.'

'Ten.'

'He was very definite.'

'Ten.'

'Thirteen would be the very, very lowest,' said Ball, cheeks beginning to wobble.

'Ten.'

'He just couldn't,' said Ball, half choking. 'It's just not on. Not there. He mustn't lose.'

Sebastian laughed, crossed his long legs and turned ash off his cigar on the heel of his shoe. It looked somehow like Ball being skinned alive. Philip even looked away, a responsive nerve jangling at Ball's agony.

'He might, I should say only that he *might*— go as low as twelve,' said Ball.

'Ten,' said Sebastian comfortably. He sat back, smoked his cigar and stared steadily into Ball's twitching features.

'Im-possible,' stammered Ball. 'Quite. He would never even listen. I should lose a valued client—'

'Lose him,' said Sebastian. 'And me.'

Ball swallowed. Philip looked back again at the torture scene. He had a sudden urge to bash Sebastian over the head with a soda syphon, but lit another cheap cigar instead.

'Ten,' said Sebastian.

'Absolutely final—' Ball blurted desperately '—he might go eleven.'

'Nine,' said Sebastian.

'God!' snorted Philip in a hiss.

'Oh no!' Ball seemed about to burst into tears. 'No, you can't Mr. Stanley. I should die in between the two of you.'

'I'll split the difference then,' said Sebastian. 'Ten.'

Philip looked at the ceiling. Ball covered his face with his hands after dropping his hat.

'What—what shall I do?' he cried passionately.

'Go and tell him it's sold, for ten,' said Sebastian.

'He'll kill me!' moaned Ball. He bent and picked up his hat, jammed it on and ran to the door. 'Kill me!'

He heaved the door open, rushed out and left it open behind him. They heard the front door open and slam shut.

'Idiot,' said Sebastian, looking at the open door. 'Why does he go to all that trouble?'

'I don't see his client being very pleased, taking a cut like that,' said Philip, curiously.

'He is his client,' said Sebastian. 'That's his process. He pretends he's acting for Gleeson who doesn't exist. He's Gleeson, and a few other names I have known. Why he goes to all that trouble when he knows I know I can't say, but he always does.'

'He knows you know?'

'Of course he does. He's been doing it for years.'

'By the way, what is it you've bought?' said Philip, looking only casually interested.

'Merchandise,' said Sebastian, closing the subject.

Philip let it stay closed. He was more interested in how 'Mr. Gleeson' was going to be paid. Anyone who took a cut from fifteen to ten in thousands could not be dealing in honest stuffs, and therefore it followed that that one would be unlikely to accept a cheque.

It would be cash, and Philip was keenly interested in where it was going to come from. The Bank was out, as the payment by cheque was out, for dishonest deals should be untraceable to be effective in the long term. And Sebastian was a long-term operator.

That was one statement that could be taken as fact.

'Has he been doing this play acting for long?' said Philip, casually.

'Some years now,' said Sebastian. 'We have done quite a bit of business together. He invented the game to hold out against me. At the start he won because I believed there was a genuine seller behind him who wouldn't budge. Then I got wise to the trick and let him know it, but it made no difference. He goes on doing it. You can see that he's a lunatic.

'There are two things about him that have

always struck me adversely,' Sebastian added, looking at his cigar in a thoughtful, almost calculating way. 'One, he picks his nose with his little finger, and two, he is very rich in actual cash.'

Philip looked up sharply.

'Why adversely?' he asked.

'I don't think he should have it,' said Sebastian, pleasantly. 'I think that I should have most of the money in the world. I know how to enjoy it.'

Philip got up, walked to the window by the piano and looked out into the twilight in the front gardens.

'Just how do you enjoy it?' he asked. 'You don't seem to do much, staying here alone with a part-time housekeeper popping in to do some of the house.' He turned round. 'What happens to the rest of the house?'

'It stays as it is,' said Sebastian, coolly. 'What else can it do, all by itself?'

'Why don't you get somebody to share it?'

'I need neither company nor money for having it. I am content with what I do, but not with what I have.'

'A greedy old sod,' said Philip, with a show of anger.

'You don't approve?' said Sebastian, leaning forward and peering round the wing of the chair.

'I can't understand how two such unalike characters can have come from the same family,' said Philip. 'You're a disgrace to the memory of my mother.'

Sebastian sat back again.

'I have heard that Victorian melodrama is becoming popular again,' he said, pleasantly. 'Is that what you write? You speak it well. Ham, they used to call it. Once I went to the theatre a great deal.'

'You won't mind if I go for a walk? I need some fresh air.'

'Drown yourself,' said Sebastian, generously. 'I shall play myself some music. I compose, you know.'

Philip went to the door and out into the hall. As he opened the front door the notes of *Tea for Two* came from the piano with much trilling and rolls up and down.

Med appeared quite suddenly, it seemed, in the shadowy hall behind Philip.

'Not going?' she said.

'Just a short walk.'

'Oh. But he does upset people so. I was wonderin'.'

'Are you saving on juice? It's dark out here.'

'If a light is on before it's pitch, he'll be raisin' the devil.'

'I see.'

With the door open and the smell of the dusk of the May evening Philip suddenly felt he must get out of the house, run, fast, before it got him.

His imagination was playing on his guilty

conscience. And yet not that alone. He had come to do evil in that place, but it seemed that evil was already there. He felt that it might be greater than his own small, unpractised variety could cope with.

In fact, at that moment on the threshold he felt for the first time that something much darker, grimmer than he had invented was gathering around him, like a silent, menacing host.

For the first time he felt that his will would no longer rule the game that was coming. He felt he might be made to obey another's will.

If that happened, the game was lost.

And so was Philip Stanley.

2

He walked out and down the steps. Once on the drive, feeling his shoes beat the gravel and the cool of the air, touching his face the feeling faded. If not confidence at least resolution returned to his uncertain soul.

He walked along the Avenue to the far end where a large pub looked on to the common and its guardian rank of horse chestnut trees. The candles on the trees were beginning to shoot. The year had been warm from January, and that night, Philip felt, was even hot for spring.

There was a beer garden to the front of the

pub, strung with fairy lights. He got a pint of beer and sat down facing the common and the trees growing black against the coming night.

As he sat there thinking, a man came and sat at his table.

'All right, then?' the man said, grinning.

Philip started uneasily, then recognised the fellow as a Cornish engineer who had stayed at the same hotel as he had, weeks before.

'Fine, thanks,' he said.

'On another job here?'

Philip might have been struck a blow. In the next second or two he tried desperately hard to remember what he had told this man before and could not. His face went cold, then hot and clammy.

'Yes,' he said, and drank.

The pulses in his temples began to beat, squashing his brain in between them.

He could not remember what he had told the man, only weeks before. His memory just stopped, locked solid.

'Very interesting, your work,' the Cornishman said. 'Does it affect you much, this change in the budget?'

The budget? What in hell did the budget have to do with what he had told the man?

He strained to remember, but the harder he tried the thicker the blanking-off curtain in his mind became. He felt a stream of panic. He was like a man beating at the door of a prison suddenly shut on him.

He switched his mind to concentrate on behaving normally.

'Not a lot,' he said. 'We get used to these changes.'

'I thought it might increase the offence rate, as they say,' said the Cornishman.

'Bit early to tell,' said Philip, wiping his face. 'Hot tonight.'

'Very good weather,' said the Cornishman. 'It'll be raining at home. Where are you staying this time?'

'I'm thinking of pressing on. Want to be back at the office first thing.'

'Office?' said the Cornishman, surprised.

Another cold wave washed through Philip's frightened being, leaving his face hot and damp.

'I shouldn't have thought you operated from an office,' said the Cornishman.

'One must have a base.'

'Oh, of course.' The Cornishman remained puzzled.

Philip's struggle to remember turned into a weakness almost like letting go the edge of a cliff and hoping it would be soft somewhere else, and he funked altogether.

'I must go,' he said, and finished his beer. 'See you sometime.'

'All right then? Don't stew 'em!' The Cornishman laughed.

Philip laughed but suddenly felt his jaws had seized. He turned away and almost stumbled, going through the gate on to the pavement of the Avenue.

'Bloody hell!' he said softly, desperately. 'I couldn't remember. I couldn't even remember!'

He walked away without any purpose but to clear his head. Almost as soon as he left the beer garden he remembered what he had said to the Cornishman. That made it worse.

If ever an enquiry was made later and he went blank like that he'd have had it.

A sort of panic came again, and his mind twisted like a rabbit in a trap.

Then he thought: But I haven't done it. I don't have to do it. I could walk away now and nobody would follow.

That heartened him. He walked straight on back to Fairfield.

He rang the bell and stood there on the steps, waiting. For some reason he felt better, stronger with the smell of the place in his nostrils again. He remembered what he had meant to do. He remembered how strong he had felt when he had decided and planned it, and he began to feel the same then.

Nobody came to answer. He rang again. It seemed very quiet afterwards. The noise of the town was somewhere far off in the sky behind him. All round him was a velvet quiet. For a moment he thought he could hear a heart beating somewhere in the softness.

The door opened. Med was there. The hall

behind her had only one small table lamp near the stairs. Like a candle in a naughty world, he thought. It was almost swallowed by the shadows of the hall.

'Have you been waitin' long? I can hardly hear the bell, where it is in there.'

He went in. She closed the door.

'Where is he? Asleep?' he said.

'I never know where he is for sure, not when he isn't there where he's supposed to be.'

'Does he often—disappear?'

'Sometimes. It's usually after he's been doin' some business.'

'Gone out?'

'Oh no. Not gone out. 'Tis a big house, one way and the other. He gets himself lost. 'Tis not my place to look, nor me inclination, neither.' She laughed.

'He doesn't seem to bother with his guests.'

'Oh, he's not the kind to. If he ever has any it's just to amuse himself by bein' rude to the poor devils. I've seen enough, and I know this disappearin', too. Do you want to go to bed? 'Tis no use at all waitin' around for him. When he goes like this he might be hours.'

'I'll go to bed,' Philip said. 'It's late, anyhow.'

'Some might think so,' she said and smiled. 'When you go up you can switch on the light to see you up, then switch it off when you get into your bedroom.' She smiled again.

'You must be joking,' he said. 'Why doesn't

he have trip switches like inside the fridge?'

'Ah, but 'tis he that's payin' the bills, you know.'

She smiled at him. She looked beautiful and enticing in the soft pink light of the single lamp. He went to go up the stairs, then caught her round the waist and went to kiss her. She smacked his face so that he drew back very sharply.

'I can see them comin' from hours before,' she said and shoved him away so hard he struck his back against the newel post and hurt his shoulder blade.

'Okay,' he said, turned and went up the stairs.

At the top he stopped and looked down again. She was there still, smiling up at him. He had a sudden desire to go back down and fight it out if need be; then he remembered that somewhere in the house the old man was hiding. Perhaps even only a few feet away.

He switched on a light, opened his bedroom door, turned the light on in there and then switched the landing light off. As he closed his door behind him he felt suddenly ashamed and angry. He was doing precisely as he was told.

The poison was in already.

He sat on the bed and thought it over, but all he could think of was the old man hiding somewhere in the shadows of the house.

Of course, he realised, that was what the old man did it for. Perhaps he always did it when guests were there. It stopped them looking round the house on their own. It was a sound psychological principle of keeping the fright on the wayward and holding him stationary with his curiosity eating him out from the inside.

He had brought no luggage, but a shaver and a flask of brandy in his raincoat pockets. The weight made the coat swing unpleasantly when he carried it, but later comfort balanced up.

He poured a drink into his tooth mug, turned the light out and stood looking down through one of the huge windows to the lights of the Avenue beyond the house trees.

They gave a blue light enough to see by.

Of course, he decided, theatrical it seemed, but that was what the old man was up to; creating the impression that he was watching his guest from somewhere.

Philip swallowed the drink, undressed and got into the great bed. At first it was comfortable and he lay there thinking of how he would have to change the course of the influence in that house, once he was sure where it came from.

The business of the lights and orders about same had come from Med, but she could, with her impish Irish sense of fun have made it up for a laugh at him.

And then he realised that by far the best thing he could do was muck along with them and their peculiar ways, and take their orders and make them think they held the reins. It was best always to take the long slow curve with that sharp turn at the end, when the watcher expected you to go on by and you came up behind him.

The important thing was to wait unsuspected until the deal with Ball came off. By watching details Philip should see then where the cash was going to come from. And wherever it came from should indicate where the rest of this purchasing material was lying in the house.

A point which occurred to him then was surprise that none of the fiddle dealers Sebastian did business with had organised a burglary at Fairfield. Surely there wasn't really honour among thieves?

It was a small disturbing thought, one which made his uncertain nervous mind uneasy about his prospects. But it helped him to decide that long, careful study of this whole scene was necessary before he jumped at anything.

It was not quite as easy as it had seemed a few hours before, but the real possibilities remained, if anything, stronger than before.

He felt hot and restless as thoughts and desires kept coming and going. He began to get Med mixed with the necessary plot and it seemed that she was liable to get in the way of its working.

He got up, feeling hot, and went to the window. He stood a moment looking out at the lights and the reddish glow of the town in the sky beyond. He lit one of his thin little cigars and stood longer, staring out at the slight movement of young leaves against the Avenue lights.

Standing there, looking out at the lights of life, things seemed easier. He smoked awhile, then put the cigar out and got back on top of the bed.

It was dead quiet in the house. He tired of worrying about his scheme and the details and the difficulties that seemed to appear and vanish again, and thought of Med.

The door handle turned, the door opened. Startled, he sat up on the bed.

He could see that it was Med who came in, but as she closed the door he could not see if she was wearing a coat or a dressing gown. Whatever it was, the slipped it off and just threw it somewhere across the room, and he could see she was nude.

'Don't get up,' she said. 'I'll lie down.'

She came to the bed and got on it, then laughed and got an arm across his chest and shoved him back flat on the bed.

'You can't expect me to stay alone when the old man's in a hidin' mood,' she said. 'And happy I am to say it coincides with that terrible empty feelin' I get for a widow's comfort.'

During one of the intervals she lay on her back and he rested on an elbow watching her.

'You look like the snowy mountains of

Mourne,' he said.

'You're a rare one for talkin' flab,' she said. 'If you're thinkin' an Englishman can please an Irish girl with talk, you don't understand what comes to the part of it. Talk of the Irish is music, and talk of the English is like listening to a concrete mixer with a lisp.' She laughed with him, and then began stroking, as before.

'What do you think of him—the old man?' she said.

'I think he's a greedy old crackpot.'

'No harm though, would you think?'

'Not really, I suppose. But you should know.'

'I never really could make me mind up. It's one of those opinions that's always goin' to and fro in you. You know?'

'I know. It keeps the interest.'

'What did you come for?'

'Like I told you this afternoon.'

'Then why do you stay on?'

'Like you, it's going to and fro in my mind. In the end you persuaded me.'

'You're a big fat liar,' she said. 'And if you think I'd put myself out to do some persuadin' I'll show you who's master right now, boy.'

At three a.m. she tightened her grip round his waist and hissed.

'The hell, he's out there! Just breathe.'

They lay still, listening. There was a sound like someone shuffling along the landing in carpet slippers, but it was very soft. It went away, swallowed by the enveloping quiet of the house.

She laughed softly.

'Whenever I stay he does that, the old goat,' she whispered, 'I locked me room, so what the hell?'

At five a.m. she was lying with her head on his chest.

'Ferdam,' she said, 'this is a fine way for a widow housekeeper to find herself wakin' in the mornin'.' She laughed.

Philip hardly felt like waking at all, but she soon made him.

During the morning after Sebastian had complained about every item on the breakfast because of his teeth, throat, burning tongue, sickness feelings and something about his neck glands which gave him lockjaw or thereabouts, Philip met Med in the hall again.

'You've no need to worry. He's like that,' she said. 'Anybody but me would have pulled his old tripes out a year or two back. Me, it makes me laugh. And don't go lookin' at me like that. I've me work to be doin' but if you'll keep your hands quiet just a while, I'll be decidin' whether to move in with you over your stay. I always admire a man with stamina, and I've come to wonderin' now if you've the same spirit in other things that might be even more important.'

'You tell me what things,' he said.

'That'll come, lover. That'll come,' she said.

'Just now I have things I must do.'

She went off. Philip went back into the study.

'I forgot to ask if you slept well,' Philip said.

'You must be a fool,' said Sebastian. 'She locked me up in the attic at ten o'clock and didn't let me out till six. Baggage!'

Sebastian thought of the carpet slippers at three a.m. and felt as if his feet had left the ground, leaving his head to roll about unaided.

CHAPTER FIVE

1

At first Philip felt alarmed without a good reason that he could point to, but then he hoped someone was lying, and that made it easier.

'She locked you up all night?' said Philip. 'What on earth for?'

'She suspects my sexual activity, thank heaven,' said Sebastian smugly.

'Does she do this often?'

'She doesn't stay often. Only when I have late guests, perhaps or like you, guests I can't get rid of.' Sebastian looked slyly at Philip.

Philip ignored the remark. There seemed no other way to play it without going, and so far, nothing had been done to build for the future. Staying was essential.

'I should have thought she could look after herself,' said Philip.

In his mind he could still hear the odd, soft shuffling of the carpet slippers going past the door of the bedroom at three a.m. If not Sebastian, then who? Another person in the house that not even Med knew about?

'What are you shaking your head for?' said Sebastian, sharply.

Philip went hot right through.

'Was I? I didn't notice.'

'You looked as though you were saying No to yourself,' said Sebastian. 'What would you say no about? Do you talk to yourself? Novelists usually do. I knew several. They used to gabble away to themselves and then when you mentioned it they always pretended they were trying out dialogue. Silly lot of sods, I think.'

'I thought I heard somebody walking along the landing outside my room during the night,' said Philip.

'You did?' said Sebastian. His look was sharp, his eyes almost shut, and he stroked his long, sagging cheek with the knuckle of his forefinger as if judging Philip's sanity content. 'Well, there is the woman, or had you forgotten her?'

He laughed and turned away. Philip got angry with the heat of his guilt.

'Why do you say that?' he cried out. 'What

right have you—'

'Don't lose your temper,' said Sebastian, turning back. 'People who lose their tempers are no use to me. Nor to themselves, I sometimes think. Why did you fly off?' He shrugged. 'I said nothing.'

Philip stood still, hands fisted in his pockets and tried to grip himself with the same strength. The idea of murdering Sebastian came particularly easily then. He could have done it on the spot and stood with his foot on the corpse, waiting to be photographed with his prize kill.

Hold it, hold it, he thought in alarm. Don't go off your nut.

He went cold then, for it was the first time, since he had begun to plot murder, that the sudden flash of fear came that his purposeful resolve, his dream, his cold calculations might not be the product of a strong mind, but of insanity.

He shook his mind like a wet dog and looked for an excuse. Med. Of course. He was nervously exhausted. That was it. Nervously exhausted, physically tired. An unwise state to get into in his circumstances.

'Have some more coffee,' said Sebastian, kindly. 'You look tired. Some idiots say coffee can help that condition. Take a gallon.'

He turned away to the windows and laughed loudly.

Philip stamped out and slammed the door

behind him, but stopped in the hall, hot blood flooding his face with increasing alarm at his unstable condition.

The letter box opened suddenly and spewed a stream of envelopes on to the carpet below the door. White envelopes, blue, dun, green, bearing handwriting, typewriting, scrawl and print.

Sebastian came out of the door behind him. He passed by, crouched down to collect the letters and gathered them up to his chest to hide their secret faces.

'I'll be busy,' he said straightening.

Philip watched him go back into the study and kick the door shut behind him. As he went a solitary letter came through the slot, a forgotten item in a big mail. Philip went and picked it up.

A cheap manila envelope addressed to 'Sarah Glover, c/o Fairfeld,' etc., in a childish sort of hand, sloping all ways, wavering on the line.

He put it on a table by the door and went through to the kitchen. Med was finishing washing up the breakfast things and did not turn round when he came in behind her.

When he put his arm round her waist she said, 'Get off!' and smacked him in the face with a wet washup mop. He stood back and wiped his face with a handkerchief.

'He said you locked him in last night,' he said.

She went on stacking dishes.

'So?'

'Did you?'

'I'm not rememberin'. It's not my day for thinkin'. That's Friday.' She laughed suddenly. 'So I did, perhaps. I don't know.'

'It doesn't matter to me,' he said, slowly.

'Well, then why go to the trouble to mention it, fordamn's sake?'

'He was shut up? I want to be sure of that.'

'He was shut up, indeed, but I never know whether it is able to him to get out again or not.'

'Then what's the point of locking him in?'

'Oh, I suppose he can't be gettin' out once I lock it,' she said. She could have been talking to herself, for so far she had looked only at the washing up or out of the window over the sink.

'Then who walked past the door in the middle of the night?'

She put the mop on the draining board, and turned, wiping her hands on a tea towel.

'I have stayed here before,' she said. 'And that's why I lock him up, for me husband did some national service in the Army once and he told me that a military man contains the enemy, not himself, for if he closes himself in, the enemy can come from any direction, but if he closes the enemy in, the enemy has to stay where he is.'

'Very interesting,' said Philip, impatiently, 'but who walked past the door?'

74

' 'Tis one of the Little People,' she said. 'They are wanderin' in the night protectin' the Irish all the time.'

'A ghost,' said Philip, and laughed.

'And what's the matter with a ghost, then?' she said, turning on him angrily. 'There's more to this world than occurs to the people who laugh at it. I heard those shoes walkin' before, and I know that there's nobody there, so I don't look.'

He moved closer.

'You were scared, I remember,' he said.

'Don't speak through yer teeth to me. What if I was? My feelin's is me, and if they jump I jump and because I know that we get on together and I'm not ashamed of what I feel or go lookin' for excuses, like you.'

'Like me?' he said, sharply, alarm rising again.

'Well, aren't you the little scared one half the bloody time?' she said, with a smile of contempt. 'What you think is behind yer, God knows, but your shoulder must be wearing out for bein' looked over.'

He stood back, colour draining from his face, and then sat down by the table and looked up at her.

'Is that what I look like?' he said, as if he had given up a fight.

'Well, you're a namby, aren't you? One smack in the face and you give up.' She turned away to hang up the towel. 'I'm thinkin' you're

75

not much good to me. 'Tis more than a bed jumper I want.'

He sat back, watching her, and then fumbled a packet of small cigars from his pocket.

'What do you mean?' he said.

Med looked in a mirror hanging by the cupboard door.

'Perhaps I'm wonderin' myself,' she said. 'But when I have a new man, you see, it always starts my mind thinkin' on things, new things, things to change, if you know what I mean. I don't always want to be takin' the part of a widow-housekeeper, and when I have a man taggin' on that's new it makes me feel new. It makes me think that things ought to be gettin' better for a woman with my charms and—guts, you might say.' She turned and looked at him. 'But every time I start pushin' a new man, he gives way, sort of like when you prick a balloon and just whistles off with the speed of his own fear.'

He lit a cigar. The smoke steadied him. A sudden thought came into his mind; the second time he had had it about her, but this time it was clear, like something written down.

She was after the same thing that he had come for. It was not such a shock, after all. It explained why she stayed on.

'What do you want me to do?' he said. 'Kill somebody?'

She laughed and walked away.

'I've got shoppin' to do,' she said, and went out.

He stayed thinking, his thoughts growing steeply more depressing. He began to feel his whole scheme being taken out of his hands. The scheme would go through, perhaps, but he was to be the tool, only.

While he still sat there Sebastian came in.

'Where's Med?' he said.

'Gone shopping.'

'You are quite comfortable?' said Sebastian. Philip stared.

'Thanks,' he said.

'I'm afraid if you're not,' said Sebastian, 'there is a danger that you might not stay.' He chuckled.

'It seems to be your morning for the funnies,' said Philip.

'Believe me, no,' said Sebastian, as if he had never thought of making a fool of his guest. 'Oh, and by the way, you'll be pleased to hear that John Ball will be joining us tonight. You were rather impressed by him, were you not?'

Philip carefully ground his cigar end out on its empty packet.

'I was horrified,' he said.

'Good. Then you should begin to enjoy my point of view.'

Philip stood up.

'I am enjoying the whole visit,' he said carefully. 'It's the first time I have ever stayed in a private lunatic asylum.'

'We are delighted you were able to join,' said Sebastian, and held out his hand.

Philip felt his head beating with a rage which increased with the thought that he was being reduced hour after hour; reduced, shrunk, degutted almost.

2

The idea that he himself was doing the shrinking came during the afternoon, when he walked the Common, trying to decide whether to give up the scheme and go and be free again, or stay and get control of himself.

To go seemed tempting, for freedom and ease of mind were tempting, but, walking fast and aimlessly, his urge towards Med became suddenly very strong. He was surprised, and stopped. And the more he thought, the stronger the urge became.

He sat on a bench to think over this discovery, for it was a discovery to find that lust had grown into something that felt of deep importance. Something about Med that was a part of him. Something they had so much in common that held him with a new feeling. Not love, not lust—need, perhaps. Something in her he needed for his own strength.

Perhaps he needed her to get through with this plan. Perhaps all along he had lacked the final guts, and it had been that subconscious knowledge which had made him doubt, shaken his nerve, made him realise that she had the complement he needed now.

If she had the same idea as he about Sebastian, then it might be a certain success to join forces for that purpose.

It almost gave him a sense of great relief to think that the onus of this very big experiment might be shared with another.

He decided to go back, take the risk and open it out to her.

When he got back to Fairfield he found nobody. It was the time of Sebastian's sleep and the kitchen quarters were empty. He went up to his room, uncertainty growing again because of the pause straining his determination to let it all out.

He laid on the bed for awhile and tried to think it out all over again, but tiredness beat the fear out of him and he fell asleep.

When he awoke she was shaking him and saying something that did not penetrate his fuddled brain.

'What's the matter?' he said, raising himself on one elbow.

She let go and sat on the edge of the bed.

'Did he tell you the man Ball was comin' tonight?' she said.

'Yes.'

And then he thought, by heaven, yes! Ball! He must be coming to collect the money, the ten thousand pounds—in cash. Or was it too soon after the brow-beating bargaining for him to oblige?

Sebastian wouldn't have told Philip to go and witness the handing over of such a sum. It would present to the staying guest the fact that he had such moneys in the house, and it was highly unlikely that he would do that.

'The old bastard,' she said, staring at the window.

'Why? Does he come to dinner?'

'No!' It was half laugh, half snarl, a contemptuous sound. 'He wouldn't sit around with that specimen of a—'

'That's strong,' said Philip, shaken.

'I feel strong,' she said. 'No, when he comes 'tis always business, and then it has to be late and there has to be plenty of drink about and nothin' else, specially people.'

'Then why did he tell me?'

She looked at him, her eyes blue as pools and as full of secret, unreadable meaning.

'That would be interestin' now, wouldn't it?' she said, looking away again. ' 'Tis funny, you know, but he seems to get on with you. I never known him like this with anyone else comin' here—not a feller, that is. Only too eager to get rid of 'em, but not this time. Well, there's only one reason the old bastard would have, and you know what that is.'

'No. What is it?'

'He wants somethin' of you. He wants you to do somethin', perhaps it is.'

Philip lay back and looked at her.

'Do you mean that?' he said.

'I've been studyin' the old bastard, now, haven't I, for quite some time now? He's wantin' somethin' of you and it's to do with Ball. Now what in hell would he want there?'

'What do you want to know for?' He smacked her arm.

She looked at him and smiled slowly, almost thoughtfully.

'Guessin's a good game,' she said. 'I keep guessin' what you came for and why you're stayin', bein' insulted all the time and takin' it like you are. Anybody'd think you were bein' paid to take it.'

'Guessings a good game,' he said. 'I guess you're here because you've thought of a way to get Sebastian's money.'

She laughed contemptuously.

'His money? Did you ever think of a way of gettin' it out of his tight fist?'

'You must have thought of a way,' he said.

'Fordamn! The only way to make him give up a penny would be to do him in, and then you'd better be waitin' a while to be sure he isn't goin' to send his ghost after you.'

'Do him in?' he said. 'Was that what you were hinting at yesterday?'

'You must be imaginin',' she said.

'What's so awful about it? He's over seventy, had a good time, enjoyed money.'

'To be thinkin' of takin' a person's life,' she

81

said, turning her head slowly to look at him. 'You'd never be thinkin' such things.'

'You told me to think them.'

'Would you?' she said. 'For me?' she laughed and got up. 'Somebody must be crazy. I could get all his money by marryin' him tomorrow. Did you never think of that way of doin' it?' She went to the door and turned as she reached it. 'My godfathers! There's some big bloody idiots about. I begin to think you've never opened your little eyes yet.'

She went out and shut the door firmly behind her.

Philip lay quite still staring up through the bed fringe to the ceiling, his inside turning over with sickness. He felt like a little boy again, kicking at the door that imprisoned him. He even felt like crying with rage.

After a while he went and took brandy in his tooth glass. It burnt his throat and made him feel he would enjoy taking her throat in his hands and watching her face when she realised he was killing her.

Then he pulled himself together, cleaned up and cooled off. Once cool he felt uneasy at the sort of imagery that kept coming into his head. It was not usual, but then of course he was on an unusual mission. These mind pictures were merely the reaction to tension, and the strain of unusual watchfulness.

He went down to the study when Med was laying table and helped himself to Scotch.

'Enjoyin' yourself?' she said.

'Yes. You said I'm an idiot, anyhow.'

'I don't mind you,' she said. 'You'd not be bad, for a while. I reckon I could put a bit of hard in you so you'd not be scared all the time of doin' somethin' you didn't mean to.'

She went out. He would have followed and grabbed her but heard Sebastian bawling in the hall.

'Move, slut! Some of us have not the time to hang around with thoughts to smile over. I'm hungry.'

He came into the study and shut the door. Philip looked at him and again felt he would have pleasure in closing the threescore years and ten account.

But his mind was sharpening as he thought how Med was riling him, and he tried to see a reason, and there occurred a simple key.

'Why did you never get married?' he said.

Sebastian went to the window, looked out, then turned back.

'Why ask that?' he said.

'I wondered. Why didn't you?'

Sebastian laughed.

'I did,' he said. 'She's still alive somewhere.'

To Philip the room seemed quite unreal, and he drank in a gulp to bring back the perspective.

'I thought you said Ball would be here,' he said switching quickly. He stroked his jaw and felt a fuzz patch. The shaver was getting careless. It needed a new head but it cost a bottle of Scotch. He would have to take more care about that thatch at the corner of his jaw.

'Ball will be here,' said Sebastian. 'But not until much later. How do you find it here?' He smiled at the piano as at a knowing accomplice.

'It's a change for me,' said Philip, almost fiercely. 'Remember my mother just died, my wife took another man. I haven't to be very fussy to find a pleasant comparison to my former lot.'

'You seem to be one of the born unfortunates,' said Sebastian with satisfaction. 'I have lived for seventy years and learnt a good many lessons. One of them is that people who are habitually unlucky have never had the sense to see that luck is something you work for, not hope for.'

Med came in with a trolley with the dinner on it. Sebastian looked as she set the plates.

'Steak!' he said incredulously. 'By the Lord Harry, steak!'

Philip looked away, his mind suddenly filled with the horror of listening to the clacking of the plastic teeth set for a further half hour.

'You said you liked it yesterday,' Med said.

'You bloody bloated—'

'I'll smack it to your face if you talk to me like that,' she said. 'And it'll make a change to have exercise for your jaws except with talkin'.'

She went out but shouted just before she

shut the door. 'You'd best enjoy it, for it's cost ye a bloody fortune, I'm tellin' you.'

Philip sat down and had a wish he could work his ears so that the drums would shut till the meal was over. At least he need not look, for in looking it seemed that Sebastian was masticating both steak and teeth at the same time.

Curiously, Sebastian sat down and made no fuss. Apart from the clacking, sucking and gurgling, the long exercise of his apple seemed to indicate that he enjoyed it.

Philip's thoughts turned into a new alley running round what was becoming an old subject.

'Did you tell her you enjoyed it last night?' he said.

Sebastian grinned and his apple slid right up and right down like a yo-yo in a stocking.

'She knows when I do and when I don't,' he said. 'We are very much en rapport, which means that as we each have a gun we don't fire.'

Philip felt suddenly angry and frustrated that he found himself out on a branch alone, outside the Med-Sebastian axis.

And yet still the real idea that mattered to him did not occur.

Sebastian got up, as before, leaving the guest to sit on.

'Ball will be here about eleven,' he said. 'I think you would be interested in the conversation. It might even be the beginning of your working to be lucky. What more can a devoted uncle do for a delinquent nephew?' He smiled. 'Please do what you like, but I do want your company at eleven. That is, of course, if you don't mind.'

And suddenly Philip swallowed anger as a bright flash of opportunity lit his brain. It was only an opportunity, and sense might say that it would not come off; but Sebastian was not orthodox.

Philip stood up, putting on a scowl.

'If you want it,' he said. 'I'll be back by then.' He went out into the hall and saw Med there standing by one staircase. She pointed for him to close the door, which he did and then went to her.

'Where are you goin'?' she said.

'Just a walk.'

'You'll be back when he comes?'

'I said I would.'

'When is it to be?'

'After eleven. Why?'

'I want to know for sure,' she said. 'What's he doin' in there now?'

'Waiting for you to clear.'

'Nothin' else?'

'No.' He watched her. 'What are you up to? Going to marry him and get his money?'

'That's a long way round.'

'He's married.'

'I know that. Now listen. You go out, and

86

you come back by the trades' door in a half
hour. Now, you'll do that, won't you? For me,
Mr. Stanley?'

CHAPTER SIX

1

'You want me to seem to go and then sneak
back,' Philip said. 'You tell me why and I'll do
it, perhaps.'
'I'll be tellin' you when you come back, little
feller,' she said. 'Now go on. The back door,
don't forget.'
She pushed him towards the front door,
turned and went off towards the kitchen.
Philip hesitated, and then left the house. All
the time of walking along the Avenue he tried
to think of what she wanted, and quakes of
fear passed through him as he thought that it
might be the murder he had come to do.
He still felt that he could do it, but it must
be in his own time, when everything had been
carefully worked out and he had allowed for
every possible slip. But the idea of being
pushed into it made him frightened. He did
not want it that way at all.
He walked into the same pub without even
remembering the Cornishman from the night
before. It was only after he had bought a drink

at the inside bar that he turned round to find a seat and remembered the man.

It was a nasty shock to his system that he should have forgotten the man altogether. It should have been his first concern, to avoid the keen, humorous eyes of that man. It was one more thing that reminded him of his weaknesses for murdering.

All famous murderers had become famous because they had forgotten something.

He saw the strings of fairylights shining out in the dusky garden and turned his back on the scene and went into a bar right at the back of the inn and sat down in a pew by an empty table. There he went on thinking fearfully of what Med wanted him to do.

Sebastian's marriage had upset everything. It was an unknown factor which upset Philip's main scheme but made Med's rather too plain for comfort.

A wife somewhere made him second in line as legatee, and perhaps fourth or fifth, if there had been any children. Philip felt sure there were none. He felt that one thing Sebastian would have mentioned would have been an offspring.

No, he felt sure there were no middle-aged toddlers waiting for Daddy's death. He felt sure that any children, following father's footsteps, would have been on the sponge morning, noon and night, just as Sebastian himself had been to his sister.

Philip felt a little cheered by this reflection, and bought another large Scotch. A few people began to come into the bar. Philip feared to look in case one should be the Cornishman, but no one approached him.

With the warming drink rising in his blood he felt his confidence as a murderer return. He began to review his earlier plan with favour but a little modified then by experiences he had had at Fairfield from the inside.

Then John Ball, prostitute's friend, came to the front of his mind. And suddenly, John Ball seemed like a friend to Philip as well. He seemed like a gift of unimagined splendour.

The realisation of this beneficence caused him to buy one more large Scotch, by which time the stipulated half hour was up and over.

Philip got back to Fairfield almost an hour after leaving. Med was in the kitchen, sulking. When he went in she turned as if to bawl him out in a great flood of rage, but it changed abruptly into a look of big, blue eyed alarm.

'Yer not drunk, are you?' she said.

'No.'

'Well, that's somethin'. Now look, come a few minutes he'll be goin' upstairs now. You follow and find out which room he goes to. It's to the top somewhere, but they're always locked and I cannot find which it is he goes to.'

'What do you think is in wherever he goes to?'

'Money. What else would we be lookin'

for?'

'Okay. All right. I'lll look for you, but I want to know something first. How long have you known he was married?'

'I'm never for sure he is. He's such a bloody old liar you can't tell. It could be a fib he's made up as a self-defence.'

'Have you ever heard of any children?'

'Oh God, no. There never would be. He hates women. If there was ever a wife it wasn't for what she got, but what she owned. He's a man's man all right, but though he hates women he likes to frighten the daylights out of them. That's the kind he is. I'm makin' no mistake about it.'

She went to the door, opened it slightly and looked upwards.

'He'll be goin' in a minute.'

'How do you know he hasn't gone already?'

'He always leaves a little light up on the landin'. You'll know by that if he's gone by. Then upwards there's a lantern hangs on a nail. He takes that and goes on, but where I never found out. That's where you come in, darlin'. Go forth. Be brave. Take your little heart out of your mouth, now.'

She opened the door and pushed him.

'Wait near the stairs there,' she said, and closed the door.

As on the previous night, the one reading lamp over by the study door did little to relieve the general gloom. Pools of darkness by the

90

side of the stairs were enough to hide three or four watchers. Even Philip felt safe from detection—until Sebastian came out of the study.

Philip almost tried a tortoise act in the darkness by wishing he could shrink into his suit and disappear.

Sebastian came out into the hall, turned and locked the study door. While slipping the key into his pocket he looked slowly round him.

It was almost as if he expected to find someone there in the shadows, watching him.

He moved forward when Philip feared his lungs would collapse under the strain of holding his breath any more. When he did let go into a handkerchief to muffle the noise, he felt the pulse in his temples begin to hammer.

Sebastian went to the stairs opposite the ones Philip hid by. At the bottom he stopped and looked back in the direction of the kitchen. He waited a few seconds, then nodded and went on up. At the top he paused a moment, then snicked on a small table lamp standing by the stair rails. It was of very low wattage and as he moved on he went right out of the pale of it.

Philip waited, his heart thudding unpleasantly, and then he crossed the hall and went up the stairs on tip-toe. Near the top he laid down on the slope of the stairs with his head on the level of the landing then looked along the floor under the table where the lamp stood.

At the end of the landing he saw Sebastian standing by another flight of stairs, flicking a lantern on and off as if testing the switch.

A frightening idea flashed into Philip's head that this whole setup was a trap for him; an attempt to find out what he had really come for.

Automatically he slid down a stair, and then turned and looked down.

Med was standing in the shadows below, watching him.

He looked round again and moved up the last stair to look under the table again. Sebastian was going to the foot of the attic stairs, casting the lantern beam in a circle before him.

And then he decided; if it was a trap he must know what and why. If it wasn't, he was on the trail of real money in the form of translatable notes.

He got up and went to the door of his own room in case Sebastian looked back. He didn't. The light went on up the stairs, still shining after the silhouette of the man had disappeared round the angle of the stairs.

Philip ran as fast and as quietly as he could. The carpets were still thick enough to soften the sound. The attic stairs had no carpet. He could hear Sebastian's shoes grating on the bare wood.

Philip reached the bottom of the stairs and

went up to the angle. At the top he saw the light moving down the ceiling of a passage above. He crept up the stairs until his eyes came level with the passage floor, and then, as before, stopped and watched.

It was a long passage and there seemed to be a large number of doors, confused by the perspective of the corridor shrinking into the distance of shadow beyond the lantern beam.

Sebastian looked back and stayed looking back. Philip held still, terror paralysing his breath, muscles, heart. It seemed Sebastian would never move again, but would stay looking down the passage to the dark top of a head above the floor.

Philip drew back, even at the risk of the movement being seen. He crouched down, clutching the stair nose, his hands shaking.

Then he became still again. A key clicked, a handle rattled. He raised his head sharply. He saw a narrowing vertical band of light as a door closed and then nothing.

Below him the faint light from the main landing made a pale patch against the angle of the stair wall. He turned and went down again to the bottom.

Med was standing by the stairhead by the lamp, looking towards him. He went to her.

'Did you see—' she said.

'A lamp,' he said, breathlessly. 'I must have a lamp.'

'Wait,' she said and went back to her room.

She came back with a torch. 'Don't be too long. You know he must come out again. Just find which room.'

'Yes.'

He went back and crept up the stairs once more. The passage above was dark. He snicked the torch on and went slowly along, looking at the door handles. They were all brass. They all shone equally.

He tried to remember just how far down Sebastian had been when he had looked round for that last time, but could not. The end of the passage had been in darkness, so that it had been impossible to see if Sebastian had been halfway down or at the end of it.

He went right to the end. There were seven doors on one side, five on the other. And the end of the passage bent into another, with two more doors.

No wonder Med hadn't been able to say where Sebastian went when he disappeared. This was the Victorian servants' quarters and the box rooms; fourteen doors to choose from.

He turned the light out and listened. Water was trickling into a cistern somewhere above his head, but he heard nothing else.

He thought he might see a band of light from underneath a door and felt his way along with one hand lightly touching the doors and the strips of wall between. No band of light. No sound but the water trickling.

He leant against the wall and tried to see

the scene as Sebastian had gone down the passage. How many doors had he passed? Three? Four? Five? Or had he been right at the end of the corridor and when Philip ducked, gone round the angle to one of the last three rooms?

He did not know what to do. Minutes were passing. Soon Sebastian would come out again to go down and meet Ball, and he might come out of any door, in front of, or behind Philip.

Philip turned on his light again and went down to the landing. Med was still there, watching.

'Well?' she said eagerly.

'I couldn't find the room,' he said between his teeth. 'There are too many doors—'

'Damn! You can't do anythin' straight, can you? Go on, get out again and come in back through the front door.'

He hesitated, then gave her the torch and went downstairs. She went to go into her room with the torch but turned as Sebastian came down the stairs at the end. He hung his lantern to the nail in the wall then came down the landing towards her.

He stopped by her and looked her straight in the face.

'What a lying crook,' he said, then laughed and went on down the stairs to his study.

As he got there she picked a vase off the lamp table and threw it at him as he was unlocking the door. It missed, burst and starred on the floor behind Sebastian.

'I'll take that off your wages!' he called up, and opened the door.

2

Almost as Sebastian closed his door, Philip knocked at the front. Med went down quickly and opened it. As he came in she signalled him to go with her out of earshot of a possible listener in the study.

'Didn't you see any sign at all up there?' she whispered. 'A light under a door?'

'There was no light at all. I was thinking out there just now. No light, and I couldn't hear anything of him. I reckon he's got a soundproof room up there. With that you wouldn't hear anything from inside and you wouldn't see a light either.'

'Padded cell, you mean,' she said. She stared towards the study door. 'Yes, that could be it. But it doesn't help because all the bloody doors up there are locked and only he has the key.'

'Every door up there?' he said.

'Did you try any?'

'I didn't want to make a noise.'

'If he lets you in there when Ball comes, see where he gets the money from,' she said. 'He has the safe in there, but if it's there why does he go up in the attic, ferdamn's sake?'

'Maybe he just puts it in the safe when he brings it down.'

She cocked her head.

'There's the bell,' she said, and went off into the shadows towards the kitchen.

Philip turned to the stairs and made a show of just having come down them as Sebastian came out of the study and looked at him.

'Go in there,' he said, jerking his head at the open door behind him. He went on to admit the caller.

Philip went into the study. He heard talking out in the hall then Sebastian came back with a stranger, a man in a quiet suit.

'This is Detective Constable—what did you say?' said Sebastian as he closed the door behind them.

'Watson, sir.'

'This is my nephew. You can say anything you want to in front of him.'

Watson looked at Philip. Philip felt a cold quake in his stomach.

'He is staying here,' Sebastian explained. 'Go on, constable.'

'A Mr. John Ball has made a complaint against you, sir,' Watson said, without any emotion.

'Has he, the bastard?' said Sebastian, almost thoughtfully. 'What complaint?'

'He said you had been threatening him.'

'State the case,' said Sebastian shortly, and started marching up and down with furious strides.

'It's really a matter between you two, we think, sir—'

'Having regard to my criminal record of throwing flower pots at passing pedestrians,' said Sebastian fiercely. 'Very well. Continue.'

'That in the course of doing some business with you, you threatened him with violence if he did not agree to your price. That is during yesterday evening, he thinks about ten o'clock.'

Sebastian stopped, sheer gaiety and surprise shining in his eyes.

'Why, how fortunate, constable!' he said. 'How most convenient for us all. My nephew was present at that meeting. He was here all the time. Consult him, constable. Consult him!'

Tricky old bastard, Philip thought, and so, in fact, did the constable.

The question was put to Philip concerning threats.

'None,' said Philip. 'It was a hard bargaining exercise and Ball finally agreed to my uncle's price.'

'What was the price for, do you know?'

Philip saw Sebastian's face behind the constable's shoulder and it was suddenly rigid.

'I don't know,' said Philip, truly. 'It was merely money that was discussed. My uncle wanted a lower price than Ball quoted. That's all.'

98

'And there were no threats?'

'None.'

'He's trying to string me up because of my criminal record,' said Sebastian. 'You wait till I see the dear fellow next.'

There were a few other questions of little importance, and the detective constable went. Sebastian saw him out and came back into the study.

'Now what's that meatball up to?' said Sebastian. 'Why lay a complaint against me?'

'It's one way of wriggling out of accepting your price.'

'It's a tediously long way round,' said Sebastian. 'So long, I don't believe it. There is something behind this.'

'He won't come tonight, then?' Philip said.

'Why not?' said Sebastian. 'He's practically got police protection. If I hit him now, he could run along with a bleeding nose and have me on the hooks. That could cost me a lot of money in damages. That way, you see, he would get his price after all.'

'Tedious!' said Philip. 'It's labyrinthian!'

'But he would win,' Sebastian pointed out. 'And another interesting point. Supposing he came here—which he will—and disappeared afterwards. There would be a ready-made case against me. How about that one?'

'You live a peculiar life,' said Philip slowly.

'I have a peculiar brain,' said Sebastian, with satisfaction.

The front door bell rang. Sebastian looked at Philip with even greater satisfaction. 'I told you I was right,' he said. 'It is invariable, my rightness.'

He went towards the door, then stopped and looked round at Philip, grinning.

'No, you admit the swine,' he said pleasantly. 'I'll be seated in exclusive splendour when he comes in.'

Philip hesitated. Sebastian went to his chair and sat down reaching for a cigar box on a small, handy table. Philip went out. The door fell to behind him as he went to open the main one.

But the caller was not Ball. It was a large pretty woman with bare brown head and wearing a white riding raincoat, which seemed more suited to a man, unless, as Philip thought, her shoulders were wider than usual. She smiled.

'Mr. Stanley?' she said.

'Yes,' Philip said, 'but not the owner of the house.'

'Oh? There are two of you?'

'I am his nephew. Visiting.'

'I see. Well, I have to see Sebastian Stanley.' She smiled again.

'Well, what do you want? He's rather busy at the moment.'

'Anybody with him?' she said.

'Not at the moment.'

'Then I'll see him now.' Smiling, she swept

in past Philip and pointed to the study door. 'In there, isn't it?'

She must have seen the door was not latched for she pushed it and walked into the study. Philip shut the main door and instinctively looked back down the hall for Med, but she was not there. Philip went into the study.

'Mr. Sebastian Stanley?' the woman said, going down towards the seated man.

'Who the hell are you?' said Sebastian, taking his cigar from his mouth.

'Eliza Wilkes,' the woman said.

'I've never heard of such,' said Sebastian, smoking again. 'What do you want?'

'I am here as an agent,' Eliza Wilkes said. 'I have come on behalf of Mr. John Ball.'

'I see,' said Sebastian, nodding. 'A trick. He does find strange ways to waste his money.'

The woman looked around, then selected a chair and sat down facing the smoker.

'A sum of money was agreed between you,' she said.

'What are you? A private dick or something?' said Sebastian casually.

'I have an agency,' the woman said.

'What about this sum of money?' said Sebastian, beginning to show restlessness.

'He wishes me to act on his behalf.'

'What makes him think I should deal with anybody else on a private matter? He must be a bigger fool than I calculated.'

'You needn't deal if you don't wish to,' she said.

'I've seen agents before,' said Sebastian slowly. 'Dozens of them. I have never dealt through an agent ever, and I never will. I am a direct man, Eliza Wilkes. I have no time for fenders.'

'Fenders?'

'They are things a boat hangs over its sides to soften the bumps,' said Sebastian. 'However, I will discuss one or two small matters with you.'

'Very well?'

'Has John Ball gone off his nut?' said Sebastian kindly. 'First he complains to the police about me, then he sends an uprated tart to try and talk me out of a deal he's already agreed to. Furthermore, my nephew is a witness to that agreement.'

'He has told me that, but he considers that he was pressed into that agreement by the two of you ganging up on him.'

'By the two of us?'

'By the two of you.'

'Very well,' said Sebastian slyly. 'Now the fact that he has sent you shows he wants to go through with this business. What makes him think that you might change my mind?'

'He just doesn't want to do it himself,' she said.

'He is jumping like a frog,' said Sebastian comfortably. 'In the first place, women don't mean anything to me. They can't persuade me. They never could. I'm not like that. I saw through the feminine game when I was very young and it's never touched me since. I am sorry to disappoint you, dear, but you are quite useless to your client in this instance. Go and tell him to come if he wants the business and stay away if he doesn't. Thank you.'

There was nothing the woman could say to that. She got up, thanked Sebastian courteously, and Philip showed her out.

'What an unsually rude man,' she said, as Philip opened the front door for her.

'He makes a science of it.'

'It's a wonder he's still alive,' she said, and smiled as she went.

Philip went back into the study. Sebastian was marching up and down in a fury.

'What in hell is he playing at?' he shouted.

'Rattling you, I should say,' said Philip.

'We have done business together for years,' said Sebastian through his yellow teeth. 'Why this, now? Somebody's put him up to something. This isn't his idea. He hasn't the intelligence of a rabbit.'

'Then how did he make his money?' asked Philip.

'Luck. Sheer blind luck,' said Sebastian, a small measure of self-satisfaction returning. He threw his half smoked cigar into the fireplace and sat down again to wait, drumming on the chair arms with his fingers.

103

Philip thought very hard then. Sebastian was shaken because his old accomplice had shown a new, unexpected side. This had persuaded him that somebody was pushing Ball on.

And it seemed to Philip, in a sudden lightening of his horizon, that Ball was being pushed and Sebastian so rattled that when the men did meet the temper would be overheated.

And Philip could think of only one reason for doing that.

But the horizon dimmed again quickly. He could not see clearly enough to decide whether everything was being put into his hands or taken out of them.

The way to make sure, he thought fleetingly, was to wait till Ball had gone, murder Sebastian, then search the place with Med for the money.

CHAPTER SEVEN

1

Sebastian went to the safe, turned and sat on that part of its top that stuck out from the wall.

'He's up to something,' he said. 'The thing is—what? Take into account he has no brains, no originality—what would you expect him to do?'

'You know him,' said Philip. 'You do the expecting.'

'He has always acted to a pattern,' said Sebastian, looking at the ceiling. 'He has always pretended he wants his own way but hasn't the strength. That's why he invented his phantom client. It gave him strength, you see. So much that he believes in that client now, though he knows I know he doesn't exist.'

'If we're playing games, let's consider it from the point where he's started to do something different,' said Philip. 'Then suppose there *is* something different. Suppose this time he has got a client. How does that alter him in your idea?'

'A startling thought,' Sebastian said. He got up and began marching about.

Philip watched him a moment, but his irritation became so great he lowered his eyes and stared at the table to try and stop his thoughts of murder. That surprised him, too.

It seemed now that every time he came closer into contact to the physical aspect of murder, his soul shrank away in disgust—or fear. Once again his mixture of anxieties flushed his face hotly. He knew he must have gone red. He remembered the detective, the cool, calm, observant detective, and knew at once that he would see and note a flush in a suspect's face.

'Why did he bargain?' said Sebastian, walking past at a quick pace.

Philip wiped his face and struggled to turn his mind to answering the question and get away from the dark fear cave in his mind.

'Bargain?' he said. 'Why did he bargain back to front? Why start high and go down when it was he wanted money to pay you?'

Sebastian stopped in amazement.

'Surely no one can be so lacking in perspicacity?' he said in wonder. 'And you? A Stanley? What on earth did you think we were talking about?'

The door opening broke the talk. Med came in.

'Where's this man?' she said. 'You don't think I'm goin' to be waitin' round all night?'

Philip stiffened and looked quickly at Sebastian. His uncle did not look at him.

'He has sent a couple of agents ahead of him,' said Sebastian. 'He is sick of the palsy, perhaps, and that takes time to smooth out. The way he does it, with brandy.'

'Well, I'm hopin' he'll be comin' soon, for I'm not waitin' around much longer, I tell you.'

'I thought you wouldn't be wanted,' said Philip suddenly.

She put her hands on her hips and looked at him.

'You never seem to know what's goin' on under your bloody nose,' she said.

Philip stood up, a sharp suspicion of something quite new and shocking pricking him.

'What is going on?' he said. 'What is all this business with Ball? Why doesn't he come? What's happened to him?'

'Nothing yet,' said Sebastian calmly. 'You're always jumping at things, my boy. I'm surprised that a case of nerves should have come down from my dear sister.'

'There's nothing wrong with my nerves!' Philip shouted.

'Ah, come on now,' said Med. 'You know you're a wee bit jumpy now and again. 'Tis obvious. But I think it's just that you're a bit sensitive. Doesn't do to be too sensitive to the world, though.'

'He's all right, just got the jerks,' said Sebastian, turning away. 'No wonder, prowling about on the top floor without a light and expecting to be shot any minute.'

He didn't look round as he said it.

Philip stood frozen for an instant, then looked at Med. Med looked at the old man's back.

'My, you have a big imagination,' she said, and laughed. 'Now what in hell would anybody be up in the top floor for when it's empty?'

'That's what puzzled me,' said Sebastian, turning to face them again. 'Although he may be a nephew of mine I can't help feeling he came here for a special purpose.'

He stared at Philip with gleaming eyes and a quiet smile on his parchment face.

'You're as mad as a hatter,' said Philip.

107

'Oh, I'll not be takin' part in any family rows,' Med said, turning to the door. 'But time's gettin' on. 'Tis a quarter to one. How much longer do you think of waitin'? I should have thought, him havin' sent two people and bein' this late now, that any sensible person would get the gist that the man ain't comin' at all. Not tonight, anyway.'

'Yes,' said Sebastian, slowly. 'Yes, you could be right. It's far too late even for him. He's up to something, that little twister, but whatever it is, it won't be tonight we'll see what it is.'

He poured a whisky.

'You don't usually drink of nights,' said Med, firmly.

'I have no special rules,' said Sebastian, and drank. 'It helps me sleep when I'm worried,' he added, going to the door past Med. 'And I am worried about Ball.' He went on to the door, opened it and turned back a second time. 'And I do hope my nephew won't follow me to my room. I am a little worried about that, too.'

He went out and closed the door behind him. Philip took a step towards Med.

'How did he know?' he said in a whisper.

'He must have seen you, you big idiot. You're not used to that kind of thing now, are you? I suppose you made too much row and warned him, so he looked.'

'You're quite sure it must be that?'

'You do look silly when you're threatenin',' she said, and smiled. 'Now, you don't possibly
108

think I told him, do you now? For what bloody reason would I be cookin' me own goose when it's goin' to lay golden eggs for me, now? Sometimes I think you don't bother to work things out before you start jumpin' all round on people.'

'What are you trying to do?'

'I'm tryin' to make you see that I'm for you and me together, and that way we can be rich. The trouble is you're so packed tight with suspicions all round you can't keep still a minute. You need confidence, love. Come on to bed. You're not so bad there.'

2

At three a.m. Philip woke suddenly and shook her.

'What's the matter?'

'He's outside again!'

They listened. The soft shuffle of slippered feet sounded on the landing outside the door.

'The old crow,' she hissed, and pushed him suddenly. 'Go and see what he's doin'. Go on!'

Philip pushed back against her hand, then got out of bed and went to the door. The footfalls appeared to be outside the door then. His hand shook slightly as he took the handle and turned it very slowly. Inch by inch he opened the door. There was light from the Avenue coming in at a window at the corner of the landing, a light patterned by the casement frame and green clear enough to show anyone moving outside the door.

He saw no one. The shock turned him cold, and then he realised the sounds had stopped. The creeper could have gone, or had stopped and was hiding.

He went back to the bed, took his dressing gown and put it on.

'Isn't he there?' she whispered.

'Can't see anybody.' he said, and went out on to the landing. He stopped by the top of the stairs and looked round him and across to the opposite flight of stairs.

The patterned light made it tricky to see any distance, but he felt he would have seen anyone moving in it, even though they could have stood still and not been spotted. He heard nothing but the slow ticking of a clock in the hall below.

The bridge of the landing crossing the hall and joining the two stair flights was empty, yet Sebastian's room was on the far side.

Then, as he stood there, listening and peering into the patterned dark across the hall he heard the steps again. The shock froze him so that his face went icy. An instant later he was hot again.

What in all hell had he to be frightened of from Sebastian? Attack? A shot? Neither.

He was just frightened of Sebastian.

He looked behind him and saw no one.

That made him more uncertain still. He heard the soft shuffling, yet still no one was moving in the corridor by his bedroom door.

Commonsense pushed him into listening more carefully and hearing the soft shuffling shuffle of soft shoes or slippers and then, looking at the floor of the landing and corridor, he saw, as he should have remembered, that the carpet was thick and fitted from wall to wall.

He went towards the bedroom door again. The footfalls stopped. He went in.

'Well?' she said.

'It must be up on the top floor. The boards are bare up there, aren't they?'

'For certain they are, but who in hell would be up there this time o' night. Not *him* again?'

'It all depends what he's got up there. It's someone walking either up and down, or to one place, stop, and then come back.'

'Well, go and look.'

'It's dark up there. You know the lights don't reach.'

She got out of the bed, picked her raincoat off a chair and put it on over her nakedness.

'I always thought it must be him, outside my door,' she whispered. 'I never thought it could be up there again. Go and look. I'll come to the stair bottom.'

She sent him off alone along the corridor and followed a way behind. When he reached the attic stairs he was in darkness. When she came to them she stopped there and laughed silently.

He felt his way up to the top of the stairs, almost stumbled at the top, clawed at the wall for support and accidentally snapped down the light switch.

Of a sudden the passage was a lane of blinding light and in terror he snapped it off again. He stood there, his eyes full of distorted purple and yellow images of the light shape of the corridor.

He opened his eyes but the flick colours were still there shifting with his sight in the darkness. And then he thought there was a vertical break in the spreading blots of the shock scene. He closed his eyes again and there seemed to be a shape in the middle of the block of light which had been the corridor.

He cursed his liver, his intemperate habits, his lack of fitness, for the ease with which he had been blinded and the way the colour blots stayed in his sight. Fit, he might have seen if anyone had stood there in the passage.

He reached out again for the switch but feared to snap it, although anyone there knew he was on the stairs and had turned the light on before.

When he realised that he knew he was not reasoning any more.

That, and the continual blasts of nerves, his imagined fears that Sebastian and Med were actually ganged together against him, melted his resolve.

He stood there in the darkness for a minute or more, then turned and went downstairs, his heart thudding so that he did not notice the noise he made.

'What's there?' she said when he got to the landing.

'Nobody,' he said.

'Did you go round the bend to the other bit?'

'Yes. Nobody's there. I put the light on.'

'But we heard somebody.'

'They must have gone. Nobody's there.'

'You sound funny. You all right?'

'Of course. Let's get back.'

He went along the landing and after a short pause she followed. They went into the bedroom. He lit a cigar and sat on the edge of the bed.

'You're shook,' she said, sitting down beside him. 'What did you really see up there?'

'Nobody. There was nobody.'

'What shook you, then?'

'Nothing. I'm all right.'

She sat a moment, watching his profile against the light outside the windows.

'Which way were you goin' to do it? When you first came, I mean?'

'Don't be a fool.'

'Well, which way? Poison in the afternoon whisky? I thought of that, but they trace it after. 'Tis no good if you get found out. You wouldn't have thought of that way, for you're clever at writin' books and work things out in the proper manner. So you must have had a good way of doin' it. Have you learnt anything since you've been here that's changed your mind, then? Is that it?'

'Med, you don't know what you're talking about!'

'Fordamn's sake, we're in it together, aren't we, now? What have you got all quiet about, then?'

'Med, I've never planned to do any murder. I might have had the idea—when I've lost my temper over his boorish manners—but no more than anybody else with a bad temper. I'm not— I've been pulling your leg a bit, I suppose.'

'Well, there's a change around,' she said admiringly. 'As me mother said, if a man changes his way of talk in the middle of talking with you it's because he does not want you to know what he's thinkin', which means that you've guessed him right.'

He ground his cigar end out in a tray but said nothing.

'One minute you say you'll do him, next you're too scared even to think of it. You told me that you would do it. Now you've forgotten you said that, haven't you?'

'I never said that!'

'You can't remember, can you? You've got a memory like a little tiny sieve. Why you're

114

always forgettin'. It's just like you've gone soft in the head since you've been here. Perhaps it's all that thinkin' about how you'll do it and not bein' able to make up your mind which is the safest way of goin' about it.'

'Shut up. Shut up!'

''Tis no good shuttin' me up, for I'm your conscience speakin' your wicked thoughts out loud. So even if I stop they'll go on inside your head, and then—'

She stopped and looked round to the door.

'What's the matter?' he said, alarmed.

Slowly she turned her head back to him.

'It's the bell,' she whispered. 'What in the devil's name, this time of night—?'

She got up and went to the door, opened it and looked out across the two stair flights. He came up behind her.

'Who is it?' he hissed.

'How can I be seein' through a door made of bloody great planks,' she whispered. 'Now look—'

She put a finger against his mouth and then pointed across the stairs.

Sebastian was coming out of a door at the head of the opposite flight, tying the belt of an old dressing gown. He seemed in a great hurry to be down the stairs and at the front door before anyone else could beat him to it.

He tripped on the way down, so great was his haste.

'Why now, you could do it that way,' she

breathed. 'A ring of the outside bell, and him come hurryin' out, and a little string tied across the top of the stairs. Now wouldn't that just—'

The door bolts rattled, and then the light from the Avenue swept in through the opening door, silhouetting a short fat man standing on the threshold. 'John Ball, for God's sake!' said Sebastian loudly. 'What the hell time's this, man?'

'I agree. I came to tell you, I agree,' said Ball urgently.

He sounded breathless, frightened. The sounds came up, clearly from the hall.

'No tricks this time,' said Sebastian. 'I've had enough of your detectives.'

'I wanted to warn you,' said Ball, all in a gulp. 'That's what I meant to do. Warn you, Sebastian.'

'Warn me, what about?'

'Not to try and kill me. Not to try anything like that.'

Sebastian stood still, a gaunt, tall figure in the gown that reached to the floor.

'Kill you? What's the matter with you? Illusions of grandeur? What on earth makes you think I'd bother, let alone take any risk for killing you?'

'It wouldn't be the first time you've done murder,' said Ball, more breathless than ever. 'I know. I've seen a lot you don't know about—'

'Come in, Johnny Ball,' said Sebastian with sudden graciousness. 'Let us have a little talk where a passer-by won't hear.'

Ball hesitated, then came into the hall. Sebastian shut the door and the two men were suddenly encased in pitch darkness.

'Don't try anything, Sebastian!'

No answer.

'Sebastian! Where are you? Sebastian!'

'I'm here, right behind you, you fool! Get in the study. You know the way.'

Ball stumbled out of the door shadow and almost fell into the study door.

'Go on, in,' said Sebastian.

Ball gasped, then straightened, opened the door and went in. Sebastian followed, head forward like an old vulture and the door closed.

'What's the time?' said Med.

'Twenty to four.'

'There's somethin' awful funny—' she said slowly and went out on to the landing. Then she turned back. 'Go down and listen at the door. Go on. It's the money we want to know about.'

She pushed him towards the stairs as he stepped out of the bedroom. He hesitated, then went down and stopped a yard from the study door. He looked back up the stairs.

As before, she was watching him, making sure he did as he was told.

He still hesitated, then heard shouting from inside the room. He went closer to the door.

'That's my bargain,' he heard Sebastian say furiously. 'Where's yours? Come on, where is it, you slimy toad! Let's have it!'

Ball mumbled. Philip could not make out what he said.

'Damn you for an idiot!' Sebastian shouted. 'You've got it in your hand. Give it to me! Give it—'

Philip heard Ball cry out.

'No, no! I warned you— No!'

There were sounds of banging and crashing. Philip drew back instinctively. In his imagination he saw brutal murder going on in that room and it terrified him. Then he realised that if he saw it, the blood, the battered head, he would be sick.

He retreated further, but from his own imagination, for it was quiet in the room then.

He remembered Med and looked round to the stairs. His heart faltered. She was still at the top looking down at him.

He went to the bottom of the stairs then stopped and leaned on one newel post. He felt exhausted, beaten.

He had come to take command of a house with only two people in it, but he had lost his own control, let alone the possibility of controlling anyone else.

The only thing that prevented Med from making him do what she liked was his own lack of guts. Nothing else. Whatever she said, he did, as far as his faltering courage went. After

118

each failure, he just went back to her again.

Sebastian just kicked him around as he pleased, and Philip did nothing about it. At the start he had pretended it would be politic to do nothing. In fact, he realised now he had never had the guts to oppose.

Since coming into the house his will had been drained out of him, and he still did not understand why or how it had been done.

He looked up the stairs again. She had started to come down but stopped when she saw him look. He went up to her.

'What happened, then?' she said.

'A fight or something,' he said. 'It makes me sick.'

'Poor wee sparrow,' she said with smiling contempt. 'What's a fight, then? You want to know about the money, don't you? Go and see what he's doin'. Put your eye to the hole. See!'

He straightened up his back against the rail. 'No,' he said. ' You go.'

'I said for you to go,' she said. 'Get down there!'

'No!'

She got him by the arm with both hands and spun him down a couple of steps. He lost his balance and went tumbling down to the bottom and lay on the floor face down, almost sobbing.

'Get on,' she said. 'Look for Mummy.'

She went down a few steps. He looked up, then scrambled away across the floor and got to his feet, breathing hard and painfully.

'Look through the little hole,' she hissed.

He knew then that she didn't want to know what went on the other side of the door. She just wanted him to do what she said.

Bruised and shaking, he went to the door but could not bend to the keyhole. Instead he leant against the angle of the door and its frame, his face grateful for the cool wood.

Through the panels he heard the voices going on. 'You agreed. You can't back out on it, you fat toad. I'll screw your bloody head off if you try that on me!'

'I keep telling you—'

'Don't waste your breath!'

'I keep telling you—'

'I'll murder you if you keep trying to twist me—'

'My client—'

'There's no client, you fat spit!'

'Yes. Yes, Sebastian—'

'Give it to me!'

Philip leant his face away from the door and eyed the green lit panels with dread.

'There is a client, Sebastian—'

'Liar, liar, fat stinking liar!'

'This time, Sebastian!'

There was a crash and thud. Philip turned and went away. She stood in his path.

'You're not goin'.'

'I can't stand it. It's nothing to see. They're fighting over—'

'We all know what they're fightin' over,' she whispered savagely. 'You get there and look through the hole. That's what I said. Get back there!'

Once more she grabbed him by an arm and slung him like a badly wobbling top towards the door. He tripped on the edge of a mat and went headlong at the door.

He struck the lower panel with a crash, then collapsed to the floor, panting and groaning. He was knocked stupid by the blow.

The door opened. He saw the lights from the room streak past his head, lining the carpet with a path, and he tried to scratch it up with his fingers of his right hand.

Dimly he heard Sebastian's voice from the room. 'My nephew! How nice of him to call. Let us have him in!'

Philip felt a cold shock as a jug of water drenched his head. It cleared his brain a little and he looked up through the water tears to the face bending over him.

It was John Ball, and he was laughing.

CHAPTER EIGHT

1

Philip tried to concentrate on the fact that his head ached and to drown his guilt in a great swamping tide of self-pity, an old weakness of his.

Ball dragged him into the study and helped him clamber up into a chair.

'Nasty knock that,' said Sebastian. 'Good job it was his head.'

Ball gave him some Scotch. Philip guzzled it as if it had been water. His dryness was extreme.

'Glad you dropped in,' said Sebastian. 'We were just talking over a little bit of business and needed a witness. Shake your head about. Clear it. I want your close attention.'

Philip squeezed his head between his hands. His brain throbbed so that he felt for a red moment that it would burst out of his skull.

Ball got a handkerchief, wetted it in cold water and wiped Philip's face with it.

'Come along, lad,' he said, smiling. 'Pull yourself together. You don't want a doctor now, do you?'

'No,' Philip said. 'I tripped on the bloody mat out there.'

'My nephew is a great sleepwalker,' said Sebastian, striding about and waving his arms at things as if conducting a tour. 'Every night without fail he walks about with his hands out in front, hoping a rich trouser pocket will get in the way. Pull yourself together, you idiot! It's only a bang on the head. Didn't even crack the panel!'

'Get on with it!' Philip shouted in a fury.

'You heard that double-crosser say he agreed to a price of ten thousand, did you not?' said Sebastian.

Ball looked at him, then at Philip.

'Yes,' said Philip, holding his forehead. The sudden rage had made his headache worse.

'You are prepared to swear to that in a court of law?' pressed Sebastian.

'You'd never have the guts to get near a court of law!' Ball cried out.

'Be so good as to shut your big fat gob,' said Sebastian. 'You would, Philip!'

'If I had to I'd have to. It's the truth, isn't it?'

'That's my boy,' said Sebastian, with considerable satisfaction. 'That's my distinguished relative. Well, you heard that, fatty. What now, eh?'

'I keep telling you it's not me, it's my client,' said Ball, in a slight scream. 'He appointed me his agent then turned down the deal I'd made. I can't help that, can I?'

'You're trying to raise the ante,' said Sebastian. 'What do you think, Philip?'

'I can't think of any other reason,' said Philip sourly. 'He might have one, but I don't know what it is.'

Ball went to him as if about to claw his eyes out but stopped short, craning forward, hands outstretched.

'It's my client!' he bawled.

'It's that famous old client Anny Onomous,'

said Sebastian.

He and Ball started to shout and yell at each other, waving and gesticulating. Philip watched in growing alarm. He thought the violence would develop into a physical brawl and was frightened of being involved.

'Settle your own affairs!' he shouted, and ran out of the room.

He stopped in the middle of the hall as if the echo of the door slamming had shot him in his tracks. He remembered Med and was frightened again.

For a moment he thought of opening the front door and running away altogether. But he could not do that wearing nothing but a raincoat.

He knew she was there watching him, but his neck seemed to be locked so that he could not look round for her and just stared at the big front door.

'Come here, soldier,' she called softly from the stairs.

He kept staring at the door. Although she did not repeat the call he kept hearing it like a thousand echoes whispering in his brain.

I'm going mad, he thought. Bloody mad.

He turned round and went to her. As he got there she turned her back and went on towards the kitchen.

Once there she switched on the light and went about making tea, keeping her back to him.

'You're as weak as a ninny,' she said, without looking round. 'You're not goin' to be any good, you know that? Every time I ask you to do something, yer little knees start knockin'—'

He ran at her, grabbed her arm, turned her so her back was against the sink and then smacked her face both ways. Just as she reached to get hold of him he got her wrists in his hands and shoved them down hard against the sink face.

'You want to watch it!' he said. 'I've had about enough of all this. Enough! I—'

She darted her head forward suddenly and bit his chin hard. He jerked back and let her go, one hand to his face.

'Bitch!' he shouted.

'That's better!' she shouted back. 'Get a bit of fire in your belly!'

She rushed at him and barged him against the table, but he got her round the waist and absorbed the full impact. She hit him and kicked his shins. He broke his grip on her and went back.

She went for him furiously, but he fought her off in a sheer panic of being hurt. Finally he threw her back against the table. She leant against it, laughing breathlessly.

He turned away to go out.

'Don't be goin' now,' she said. 'This is a big improvement.'

2

It was daylight when Ball went. Sebastian saw him out and then went through to the kitchen to get some tea. Med was there alone.

'You're early, my nosy little dear,' said Sebastian.

'I've been about a long time. Couldn't sleep, what with you two yellin' and screamin' the odds about nothin'.'

'You heard us, did you?' he said, taking up the kettle.

'There's tea made, if that's what you're lookin' for,' she said. 'Over there.'

'I will help myself,' he said, splendidly sarcastic. 'Don't get up.'

He poured tea and went and sat at the table opposite Med.

'How do you think it's going?' he said.

'I don't see it,' she said. 'He hasn't the fibre, you know.'

'All can be trained,' Sebastian said.

'He's soft and he scares easy. You might get him to it, but I doubt he'll ever do it.'

'This is nothing to do with horses and water,' said Sebastian. 'It is purely a business matter.'

'How far did you get tonight?' she said, changing the subject slightly.

'He won't agree. It worries me. It makes me think there might be some sort of client, he's so stubborn.'

'Why shouldn't he have one? That's your trouble. You've made your bloody mind up before anybody starts and you won't change it after. Johnny Ball's in for whatever money there may be lyin' about, and so it's possible he'd take a real honest to God client, now isn't it?'

'The more he sticks to a story the more you know he's lying,' said Sebastian.

'What's wrong with him stickin' to a story right now? So long as he keeps comin', it's no odds.'

'You have no finesse, Med. That's your trouble. With you it's always grab it and go. By the way, what are you going to do afterwards?'

'Oh, I shall go off and enjoy me little self. That's what it's all because of, isn't it?'

'You haven't taken a fancy to my nephew?' Sebastian narrowed his eyes and looked into his cup.

'Oh, in bed he's all right. Out of it he's got nothin'. I like someone with a bit of spirit. You'd be all right if you weren't so ruddy old. You've got all the sauce, not enough of the main course. You think I'm crude, don't you? Well, for so I am, because life to me has always been face-up with reality so I've had to choose what I can have and what I can't, but you, you have what you like because you could always pay for it. Usually that makes a man weak, but you—it's made you worse.'

'I have always had to work for it,' said

Sebastian with considerable self-satisfaction. 'There is no success without work.'

'For some there's no success with it,' she said. 'I've been wonderin' these last few days just what it's goin' to be worth when 'tis all done.'

'Concentrate on your part of the work, and the rewards will follow. Where is Philip now?'

'He went back to bed. He had some bump on his nog.'

'The fathausen is coming back tonight.'

'And what if he still says it's the client that's stallin' it all?'

'Well, it doesn't really matter, does it?'

She leant on the table and looked very straightly at him.

'You have told me everything, have you?'

'I can't tell you every detail, because these all depend on what happens at the time. We shall have to adjust as the play continues.'

'You know what? I wish we didn't have to wait so long.'

'The longer the wait the safer everything is, Med.'

'Whenever you call me by my name, that's when I get the most suspiciousest.'

He reached across the table and patted her hand. 'You can trust me,' he said.

'I'd be the biggest fool,' she said.

'For heaven's sake! What's the matter now?'

'Are you givin' me everything straight, now? Why that scrapin' about up the attic again last night?'

He stared.

'What scraping about?'

'The footsteps. All the old ghost house effects. You know.'

'I wasn't up there last night,' he said slowly. 'When did you hear it?'

'Before Ball came.'

Sebastian looked into his teacup. He looked a long time then took a drink and looked up.

'You're quite sure?' he said. 'There couldn't be any small mistake?'

'There's no mistake. I thought you were overdoin' it one way and the other.'

Sebastian sat back then and shoved his scraggy hands into his trousers pockets. He stared at Med with one eye shut.

'What's the matter with you?' she said.

'In this house,' said Sebastian, 'there's you and me and my little nephew. Is that right?'

'So you tell me,' she said.

'What do you mean by that?' he said aggressively.

'I don't know who you've got hidden away anywhere,' she said.

'You don't think that possible, do you?' he said, cocking his head and combining a benevolent smile with a sharply suspicious glare.

'It's a big house, mister, and I don't look after it all, as is part of our arrangement.'

'At this point in the proceedings, Medina,'

he said, taking his hands from his pockets and leaning across the table to her, 'you haven't started to distrust me?'

'Fordamn's sake, did anybody ever? Trust you, I mean.'

He sat back again, watching her keenly.

'What was this sound like from up there?' he said.

'Why the same as you did before. Sort of scrapin' like somebody shufflin' about up there.'

He looked at the window.

'I told you, I wasn't up there last night,' he said. 'Someone is getting in.'

She started, eyes wide.

'How do you mean? How could they?' She sat back, easier. 'You're tryin' to frighten me, you old crow.'

'I'm thinking, Med. If he came here with the idea of—you know what. I'm superstitious, you understand. If he came here with that idea, he's done precious little by himself. It's possible he has someone to help him in the business. Let me tell you a little memory.

'Forty years ago at a party—I used to have many —a young man got into the house for a bet, and he did it by climbing that big elm out at the corner of the house and clambering along a branch until he could reach the parapet. Everybody watched.

'Of course, he is dead now. Elms are very high, but they don't change much in forty

130

years. What was possible then is still possible
now.'

'But he wouldn't—he couldn't have—I
would have noticed.'

'Med, let us have everything plainly put,'
said Sebastian, leaning forward again after a
look at the closed kitchen door. 'You have
been plotting with him to—eliminate me?'

She swallowed and crossed herself.

'Yes,' she said. 'But not—'

'Has he been open about it?'

'I keep tellin' you he's a double-dyed softie.
One minute you think he's goin' to—next he's
runnin' off like a burnt cat. There's no makin'
him out, I tell you.'

'Do you think he ever would?'

She hesitated and frowned at the table.

'Funny, though, 'tis just struck me—yes, I
think he maybe could.'

Again Sebastian sat back, watching her
acutely. 'Well, that's all right, then, isn't it?' he
said.

'I don't know. You can't be sure with him.
He's such a squiddler, right at the very last
moment he gives at the knees—'

'And yet you think he could?'

She hesitated again, then nodded.

'Yes, I think he could, if pushed.'

'Then you must push him, dear,' said
Sebastian, and got up. 'Push hard. Be
relentless, vicious. Get him so that he cannot
refuse you whatever you want.'

He went towards the door.

'Just a minute,' she said.

He turned back.

'Have you ever stopped to think why he should want to do this?' she said. 'What is he to get out of it?'

'I have thought of everything.' said Sebastian. 'If he is guilty of wanting to—' he shrugged, '—then *you* have him. If he isn't, then we have him.' He smiled pleasantly, and went out.

3

'Where's Sebastian?' said Philip.

'Gone to the bank,' Med said.

'He'll miss it. It's long after three.' He sat on his bed. 'It was hell in there last night.'

'Did it frighten you? It frightens me sometimes. This fury. Even the Irish in me gets scared. You'd think there'd be rippin' apart goin' on. I've thought before he might kill Johnny Ball.'

'Kill him? What for?'

'Sheer temper. That's how most people kill others, isn't it? Not many has the courage to do it the other way now, cold, have they?'

'You keep on about that.'

'Well, why don't you do it? The longer you waitin' on the edge the worse it is. Often you never do it at all, and what then? You just get the blame for somebody else who does.'

'What!' He jumped up.

'That's just one of the things you never even thought of,' she said. 'If you'd any sort of head, you'd have taken advantage the other way round.'

He grabbed her arm.

'Who wants to kill him?' he said.

'There's plenty. He doesn't win the United Kingdom Popularity Poll, now, do you think?'

She pushed him back on the bed and got on top of him.

'Come on now, you're all mixed up feelin's and inhibitions and them things and can't make your little mind do what it wants on account of these things you were taught when you were a little boy . . .'

He forgot about murdering Sebastian.

She played him for a while and then pushed him away.

'You don't understand. You never did,' she said. 'Why do you think I'm here? It isn't because I like it. If you must know the truth, the old bastard knows something about me and he'll tell if I don't stay. So now you know!'

She got off the bed and went to the window, fastening her dress.

'You must have lived a fine kind of old life where you never came across any hard stuff,' she said. 'People are cruel, but you don't know it. People are hard and vicious and bad, but you don't know it. You can't understand why

133

anybody'd want to get her own back for things she's had to suffer and never been able to say anythin' about. You don't know what that's like. Having to live down to it—' She started to cry.

Philip lay on the bed, watching her.

'You're a liar,' he said.

She didn't seem to hear but went on crying. He sat up.

'Don't go on like that,' he said, uneasily. 'Come here.'

She turned to face him and a moment later was sobbing on his shoulder. It was so genuine it racked him.

'Don't!' he said urgently. 'Look. Stop it and tell me about it. What did he do? What's he trying to get?'

'He won't let me go. He keeps me here because he's always threatenin' to tell—'

She cried again.

'Whatever you did can't be that bad,' he said.

'It can. Yes, it can!'

'I don't want to know,' he said. 'There's only one thing you've got to do and that's get right away from here.'

'That wouldn't help. He'd tell if I didn't come back. There only one way to stop him telling—ever—that's what I meant all along.'

Again Philip felt he was going mad.

'We could do it tonight,' she said. 'And Ball would get the blame. Ball would. Everybody knows about the way they fight. Everybody knows. They hear it out in the street there—'

Quite suddenly it all seemed perfectly simple to Philip.

Ball. Of course. Ball would do it. Ball would cop the rope. Ball.

He pushed her away gently and stood up. He felt quite different, upright, strong. He wondered he had not seen so simple a plan before, but he could not remember all the things that he had thought. The blank-offs in his mind had become more frequent during his stay in that house.

'It could be done,' he said. 'It could. Yes.'

She stood away from him, dabbing her eyes, then turned her back.

'No,' she said. ' You'd best not risk it. It'll be known you're stayin' in the house—'

'Oh no,' he said. 'I'm going. Right now. Going. I'll tell him farewell and go. Tonight I'll be in the garden at the back. You signal me when it's clear, when Ball has gone. That's it. Immediately Ball goes, you flick the kitchen light a couple of times. I'll be watching. Immediately after Ball's gone.'

He grabbed up his raincoat, crammed his shaver and small things into the pockets, then went downstairs, leaving the bedroom door open. He did not look back at her.

He burst into the study. Sebastian was asleep in the chair but woke with a start and looked round very sharply.

'What do you want?' he said.

'Goodbye,' said Philip. 'I'm going home.'

'Bit sudden, is it not?'

'There's nothing I can do. Nothing you need. I came because of mother's wish, but I'm satisfied you're all right. A man who can bargain in sums of ten thousand can't want for much at seventy. Thanks for the hospitality. Goodbye.'

He went out. As he closed the door he heard Sebastian begin to laugh and fury suddenly reddened his brain. He stayed a moment with his hand on the door knob, tense with the sudden urge to do the thing there and then.

A slight shiver ran through him, and he realised it was not the time. To rush into it without any cover would be to spoil the chances of getting away with it.

He went to the front door, opened it and stepped out into the sweet smell of a late May afternoon. And the smells were specially strong. He had never realised how pungent they were.

He walked all the way to the town centre and got a taxi to the station. He argued about the fare and crossed the cab driver.

He went to the booking office and argued about the price and again, his change. On the platform were seventy or eighty people waiting for the last train on the cheap day return. He walked in amongst them very carefully and went into the lavatory and locked himself in a cubicle when the train came in.

He waited there until the next train, the first London office train, came in and let its passengers out. He left the box and joined the herd flooding out of the station. There was no ticket collector, as he knew. Tickets were collected on the train.

By seven o'clock he had left all the signs that he had gone back home by train, and felt warmly bucked about the way he was acting.

His pride in carrying out a long planned piece of subterfuge so cleanly and quickly gave him confidence in the rest of the work he had to do.

He went into the busiest pub he could find in the town where he reckoned the staff would be too pushed with faces ever to remember one afterwards.

He drank two Scotches, and then suddenly remembered the Cornishman. He left his glass and went out into the gathering dusk. But after walking a short distance he realised the man couldn't have been there or he would have come up and started talking.

His pace slackened.

There was a good deal of cloud above and it was getting dark fast as he headed back for the common. He entered it by the side farthest from Fairfield and crossed the way that was away from the path routes. It ran among bushes and small woods and he saw no one the whole way.

At the garden wall of the house he stopped and peered round into the darkness, but everything was quiet. He opened the garden door and went in to the overgrown grounds.

The only light showing at the back of the house was at the kitchen window.

The town traffic was a murmur in the night sky. The sudden hoot of an owl stopped his heart for a few seconds, but he was too determined then to let fright get him as it had done before.

He waited patiently. The kitchen light remained steady. Once or twice he thought he heard men's voices raised in angry shouting, but so faint it might have been his imagination.

As ten-forty-five was striking from a church clock the kitchen light flicked twice.

CHAPTER NINE

1

When the kitchen light flicked twice it did not come on again after the second flash. Philip made his way through the garden in darkness stumbling here and there, scratching against wild growing bushes, but hardly feeling.

His brain was cold, almost isolated from his body. His limbs went on mechanically. His determination gave him feelings of great strength, coming in waves, swelling and receding.

As he reached the door a wave ebbed and for a moment a chill cold fear edged in behind it. Instinctively he half turned to run, but heard her voice from the darkness by the door.

'Come on. Quick! Where in hell are you?' His mind froze. He could not think at all.

'Come on! It's got to be now! You'll be too late!'

The hissing voice pierced the darkness and his brain. The odd determination came again, and reasons, like strip mottoes, floated in his brain. This is what you came to do. This is the time. This is the only time when everything's set. This is the Now you planned.

He remembered the smoothness of the decoy journey back to his home, each bit of it like a pat on the back for his cool resolve. He went in, brushing against her.

'Flickin' fused the bloody lights,' she whispered. 'But he's in the hall—now. Just come out. Let Ball out. Here—'

She shoved a heavy stick into his hand.

'It's Ball's. Quick! Now, or you never will!'

She pushed him through the kitchen and out into the hall. The lights from the avenue streaked the darkness in confusing jazz. He could not see anyone at all in the light and shadow.

'There! Over by the door,' she hissed and

shoved him forward through the middle of the hall.

He had to run to save himself, only a few paces, but before he could stop he tripped over a heavy, soft sack lying on the floor and went head first towards the wall.

It was the second time it had happened. He flung his arms out to try and save his head hitting anything, but too late. He struck the wall.

In the crash and flash of light in his brain he heard a furious knocking, and then nothing at all.

*   *   *

When he saw light again he was sitting in a chair in the hall. All the lamps were on there, and the whole scene was so bright it hurt. In front of him he saw a man he seemed to know but could not place him.

He shook his head and his brain jangled. He shut his eyes with the pain. When he opened them again he saw more.

Med was sitting on the stairs, her head in her hands. He looked round to the man in front of him, then past him to a long, covered heap by the study door.

The front door was open and a lot of people were outside, about to come in. Policemen.

A cold claw got hold of his heart and squeezed it tightly. He could not breathe.

140

The man started speaking to him but he did not understand. For a few seconds he sat there staring. The man repeated.

Philip still did not understand. Another man came in with a bag. The first man said something, and the man with the bag turned to Philip. He asked him to put his head back, then put it back himself and looked into his eyes. He took Philip's wrist.

'Concussed,' he said. 'Best get him to the hospital.'

He turned and called for the ambulance men, waiting just outside the door.

'We can look after him here,' said a voice behind him.

Through the singing confusion of Philip's head the reality of Sebastian's voice penetrated. He jerked forward in the chair as if to throw himself out of it, and gave a weird, half strangled scream.

The doctor grabbed him by the shoulders and forced him back into the chair again. The ambulance men came in.

2

When he came to again, lying on a hard bed in a white room, the man was still there, sitting beside the bed. He could hear someone else in the room walking about, but did not look round.

141

'Remember me?' said the man, almost casually. Philip stared. He did remember then, but he could not speak.

'Detective-Constable Watson,' said the patient man. 'Detective-Sergeant Wills is behind you.'

Philip lay there, hearing the Sergeant but still not looking round.

'John Ball's dead,' said Watson. 'Do you remember me talking about him on a previous occasion?'

Philip stared.

'He doesn't seem to be with us yet,' said the sergeant from behind. 'Don't force it. It'll come.'

Philip stared at the ceiling. His brain was numbed, not so much with the concussion, but with the realisation that they had tried to fix him somehow.

As he puzzled over that a sort of anger clarified his mind. He looked at Watson.

'Have you arrested Sebastian?' he said.

'No. Why?'

Philip did not answer. The answer was enough, and he knew, vaguely that he should not say why. He knew he should not answer any whys or perhaps, anything at all.

He realised he had been fixed and until he knew how, he was still fixed. And if he answered any questions he might even help the fixers against himself.

'Have you arrested me?' he said.

'That depends on you.'

'What does that mean?'

'Tell us when you feel up to answering a few questions.'

It kept repeating in his head that he'd been fixed but some mental bar prevented him saying it, as if at the back of his mind he understood the danger.

'I'll answer no questions till I get let out of here.'

'We'll be waiting.'

*   *   *

At four in the afternoon he was passed fit, with a sore head but nothing cracked. He was then taken to the police station. Detective-Sergeant Wills carried the attack, Watson attending.

'You stayed with your uncle a few days, leaving yesterday afternoon?'

'Yes.'

'Was there any reason why you left?'

'It was time I went home. I only came because my mother wanted me to when she died. She hadn't seen him for a long time. He was her brother.'

'You left and caught the 6.50 train.'

'Yes.'

'How did you get back again?'

'I got off and on to another train.'

'What time was that?'

'I don't know.' He began to panic. He knew

143

he could never keep up a story which he had never had to think of before. 'What the hell am I talking about? Did they give me drugs? My head's all over the place. I didn't get on the train. I got a ticket and felt queer so I went back to the town and had some Scotch.'

'What was the matter?'

'You ought to try a couple of days with uncle. I was perforated with his drink sessions, I could hardly think.'

'Did he tell you to kill Ball?'

'Kill Ball? What in hell are you talking about?'

'All right. Play it innocent. Plenty of time. Cup of tea?'

Watson went to fetch some tea.

'Right,' said Wills. 'John Ball had his skull smashed in by a heavy blackthorn stick, cut short, which he had taken to your uncle's house as a weapon of defence. Your prints and his were on that stick.'

She gave it to me. He almost said it aloud, but stopped.

'Did you hit him with it?' the Sergeant said.

'I didn't see Ball that night.'

Watson brought in tea on a tray. They each took a cup.

'Why did you go back to your uncle's house that night?' Wills said, shovelling sugar into his tea.

'I went back to see—the woman.'

'Oh yes. One could sympathise with that.

How did you get in?'

'At the back door. She's careless with it.'

'There was a purely private motive for wanting to see her?'

'Personal. That's why I went in the back door. That's why I didn't catch the train. Just say I was hooked.'

'You went into the house. What happened then?'

'I went into the hall, fell over something and cracked my head against the wall. Next thing I knew was Constable Watson.'

'When did you grab the stick?'

'I didn't touch a stick. If my prints were on it it must have been made some other time, but I don't remember a blackthorn stick in that house. There might have been one; I just don't remember one.'

'You expected your uncle would be in bed?'

'Yes.'

'Was he early to bed usually?'

'No. The lights were all out.'

'Your uncle was in bed,' said Wills, stirring his tea. 'But Ball was in the house, with no lights on. What do you think he was doing there?'

'I don't know. He usually came in the front door, after ringing the bell. He and uncle were doing some business.'

'Amicably, would you say?'

'No. They frightened me the way they argued.'

'Violent?'

'Very.'

'Physically, do you mean?'

'Now and again, yes.'

'Of course,' said Wills. 'But Ball had always the attitude of a coward, a cringing sort of specimen. We have had doings with him in the past.'

'And you know my uncle is violent sometimes. He didn't like being pinched for it.'

'When they were arguing, was there a lot of noise?'

'Yes.'

'The woman says there was no noise that night.'

'I don't know if there was or not. I wasn't there till I fell over Ball. It was dead quiet then.'

'Your uncle is wealthy, wouldn't you say?'

'I gathered that idea. I don't know.'

'He wouldn't offer to pay you to do something you would not agree with?'

'I don't know. I wouldn't agree, as you say, if he tried to.'

'You went there to satisfy your mother's wish. Why did you stay so long? Because of the woman?'

'Yes.'

'She says that your uncle insisted on you being present when he saw Ball.'

'She's right.'

'Why?'

'Uncle kept saying he wanted a witness of the deal.'

'You don't know what the deal was?'

'I don't know what it was about, but there was a lot of money in it. They kept bargaining in ten thousands, fifteen.'

'Ten thousand what?'

Philip jerked up sharply.

'Pounds I suppose.'

'Did either of the men mention pounds?'

'I can't remember. But what else could it be?'

'That depends on what they were dealing in.'

'Well, I don't know. I don't know anything about this business. If you want to keep me here talking you'll have to charge—'

'No sooner said than done,' said the sergeant pleasantly. 'You haven't asked for a solicitor. You'll need one. Have you got your own? We'll contact him for you . . .'

'I don't see that I need one. You have two items, as far as I can see. I changed my mind about a train journey and my prints are on a stick which I might have touched any time I was in the house—'

'Ball brought the stick that night. It was his.'

She had put it into his hand. She had put it into his hand. She had put it into his hand.

But he didn't say.

'Then I don't know how it happened,' he said. 'I might have clutched out when I fell

147

over. I probably did. I don't remember clutching hold of anything.'

'You had the stick in your hand when you fell. It hit the wall and left a dent in the paper. Then you let it go as your head hit the wall and it fell back underneath you. That's where it was found. Underneath you.'

'It could have been there before I fell.'

'Yes. But the fingerprints. They are complete, fingers, side of the thumb, palm. We were very pleased with them'

'It's all been fixed,' said Philip suddenly.

'It's very difficult, fixing people,' said the sergeant. 'The edges show. And there's another characteristic about fixings. The accused always shouts about it right at the start. You, sir, are different, of course, but why now? And who? If your uncle is rich, why would he want to do such a thing? Why would he do it, anyway?'

'I want to know why Ball was there that night, on his own, in the dark, with the back door open—'

'You said she often forgot it. Or do you mean she left it for you?'

Philip hesitated.

'You'd been having it off?' said the sergeant. 'Don't worry. It's common enough. So she left it for you. And you think that Ball might have known that and fancied her, too?'

Philip's face iced over. That was a second motive, and a far, far better one than any

148

payments by uncle could have been. He had, at the back of his mind, been holding his own modest means in reserve, but with this jealousy theme it didn't matter any more.

'She couldn't stand the little fat—'

'I don't doubt that, sir. I'm saying that Ball might have decided to press his suit. She could have been quite unaware.'

Philip steadied.

'Of course,' he said. 'But what about the stick, then? If he was going to try and get going with Med—the housekeeper—why take a stick like that with him?'

'That's a point, sarge,' said Watson.

Philip began to seethe again. If Sebastian had been in bed and Ball had gone in to find Med, armed with a stick heavy enough to kill a man, what had he really meant to do?

He was hedging with himself, but was sickened by the real question he would not face.

How had she got the stick she had put into his hand?

Ball had taken it there. She had got it from him.

'Are you sure Ball took that stick there last night?' Philip asked suddenly. 'It seems to me more likely he took it there before, after he sent Watson and the detective woman the night before last.'

'What detective woman?' said Wills sharply.

'I can't remember her name, but she came

149

as an agent for Ball. He was afraid to come. Uncle wouldn't deal with her and said Ball or nothing. And so Ball came—about four the next morning.'

'Late as that?' said Watson, surprised.

'We heard the bell ring.'

'You and the housekeeper?'

'Yes.'

'Who heard it? You or she?'

'She did. She is sharp in hearing.'

'What happened? Do you know?'

'We went on to the landing and saw uncle tearing down the stairs. He was putting his dressing gown on. I thought he might trip on it, the hurry he was in.'

'He liked to answer the door himself?'

'Yes. His business was his own.'

'He let Ball in? You saw that?'

'Yes'

'What happened then?'

'They went into the study and she said I'd better go down there in case there was any trouble.'

'Was there?'

'The usual bawling and shouting, but again I got frightened that somebody was going to do some harm if it went on like that.'

'But if it always happened like that why should any harm be done? They seem to have been used to it.'

'Look here, sergeant. He carried that stick—Ball, did. He sent a constable and a lady detective—'

'Don't you remember what the lady's name was?'

'No, she did say, but I forget. She was only acting as an agent for Ball.'

'But Ball himself was supposed to be an agent for somebody else, didn't you say?'

'That's what he kept saying, but he wouldn't say the name.'

'Your uncle says there was no client. He says the deal was straight between himself and Ball. How did you get that stick?'

'I must have touched it when I was knocked silly. I don't remember it at all. Do you suggest I fought him for it?'

'No. There were no signs of a struggle. He was hit from behind.'

'In the dark?' said Philip, surprised.

A frown passed over the sergeant's face.

'Why do you say that?'

'The lights were fused when I got there.'

'They were all right when we got there. Perhaps you didn't try one.'

'No, I didn't. I knew the way.'

'To her room. Yes, of course. And as you were going to go up there you saw Ball in the hall.'

'I never saw Ball that night.'

Philip was charged and appeared before the magistrates next day and remanded in custody. He appeared twice more while enquiries were proceeding, from which he began to think that weaknesses might have appeared in the police case.

He worried then that they might turn and implicate Med. Philip did not want that. Quite strongly he wanted her to be left right out of it. For, except in moments of cold, sweating nightmare, he believed the case against him must fail. Because he was innocent.

The police case was presented before the magistrates on his fourth appearance in that court, and the defence case was reserved.

He was sent down for trial at the Assize Court on July 6th.

CHAPTER TEN

1

Philip saw his counsel several times. Charles Enwright, Q.C., was a glutinous man, fat, flabby, sucking on to facts like a leech, sucking everything out of them. That he did not approve of Philip was clear at the start, but his interest was not in Philip but in the case.

'The police have not got a good case,' said Enwright, 'but they always have a better one than the defence. A jury always thinks there is no smoke without fire, and mostly they are right.

'There are two possible motives for you

killing this fellow. One is that your uncle promised to pay you, and the other is jealousy. Jealousy is the line they'll take. It fits in more easily than anything else, and you were having an affair with the woman.

'There is also evidence that you often fought with your ex-wife culminating in your being thrown off a balcony. Newspaper reports are available. Violence, therefore, is evident.'

'I am not violent.'

'They will say you are. That is what counts; what they will say. If they stick to that line then all stories of business deals between your uncle and Ball don't matter, which is fortunate for them.'

'Why?'

'Your uncle denies there was any deal.'

'But he—'

'He says there were arguments about quantities that should be supplied for certain work. He was at one time an adviser to government suppliers. That is what they were talking about. Your uncle was not contracting to buy anything but arguing for Ball's benefit.'

Philip sat still.

'You told the police that you were fixed,' Enwright said, sitting back so that his big belly spread. 'I have the impression they regard this as an after-thought of yours. Is there anything in it that might help us?'

'I got into that house after he was killed. I was knocked out and when I came to the police were there and I had that stick.'

'You suggest Ball's murderer was still there and knocked you out?'

'Of course.'

'The woman? Mrs. Cusack?'

'No. She had no business with Ball. Couldn't stand the sight of him.'

'She said.'

'Well, how else can I tell? Yes, she said.'

'Then you had no reason to be jealous of Ball?'

'None at all.'

'You suggest your uncle was the murderer and left it to you to take over, as it were, by making it seem that you were the guilty one?'

'Who else was there? Nobody else was involved at all. I didn't see anyone else at that house but Ball—and that woman. The woman detective, Eliza Wilkes. I couldn't remember her name for a long time but I'm sure that was it.'

'There is no record in Ball's office or home that he ever employed such a person.'

'She was there the night before. She came after the policeman, Watson.'

Enwright leant forward again.

'How did you get that stick?'

'It was under me when I woke up.'

'You had hold of it. You had gripped it—hard. The prints are clear as to that. They are also several times superimposed as if you had gripped and relaxed your hand several times while you held it. I don't think the forensic people are mistaken on a simple point like that. You had hold of that stick before you were knocked out. You may forget the idea that someone put it into your limp hand and pressed the prints on. No one else could have made your hand act as the prints say it did. The story of finding it under you just will not do.

'Where did you get the stick?'

'I found it in the kitchen.'

'You said the lights were fused. How did you see it was there?'

'I had a torch.'

'Who told you the lights had fused?'

Philip hesitated.

'Nobody. I'd seen them flicker from outside. I thought that was it.'

'And you didn't try switching on?'

'No. I didn't want to be seen, of course.'

'Of course, because you were going upstairs to bed with Mrs. Cusack, which was the sole purpose of your visit, was it not?'

'Yes.'

'Then why take the stick?'

'Honestly, I don't know. One does things, without a definite reason. Specially when one is nervous.'

'Did you and Mrs. Cusack talk about your uncle?'

'Of course. I wanted to know about my only relative. She'd been there a while and knew

155

him well enough.'

'Did you ever talk with her about murdering him?'

'Of course not! Why on earth should we?'

'He was wealthy—or still is, and you, well, shall we say that even after the sale of your mother's house won't be living in luxury. In fact, the state of your affairs is lamentable.'

'I can make a living. I always have.'

'At some expense to your creditors, I would say. And that is what the prosecution will say if they are pushed to the point.

'Let me say something else that might be suggested.

'You were hard up, even after your mother died. You were wriggling. You came to Fairfield because you knew your uncle was rich—or could well be—and did so with the fixed intention of spying out the land with the idea of murdering him and inheriting as the only relative.

'That with the assistance of Mrs. Cusack that night, you were let into the house, given Ball's stick and let into a dark hall where you murdered someone you thought was your uncle and found that it was Ball.'

'No,' said Philip, shaking.

'In this case, where there is doubt and you have no record, your survival depends on going into the box. By keeping out of it, you put the jury to thinking you did it and won't face cross examination about it.

'But on present showing, your appearance in the box would very likely be disastrous. You present a problem in more ways than one.'

'The man was dead when I fell over him!'

'The woman knew you were coming that night?'

'I told you the did.'

'Then she murdered him.'

'No!'

'Either she or your uncle. Both were upstairs in different places, it seems, and you say nobody else was there but the man lying dead in the hall.

'Let us have the detail again. You waited in the garden till you saw the lights go out?'

'Yes.'

'But they flickered, and you thought they'd fused?'

'Yes.'

'As the lights had been on till then, did it not occur to you that someone might come down to mend the fuse?'

'I was excited. I didn't bother.'

'I put it to you that the flicking of the lights was a signal between you and Mrs. Cusack?'

'No, it was not!'

'And that when you went inside she gave you the stick.'

'No.'

'She must have held it with some sort of cloth so as not to upset Ball's prints. Did you notice what sort of cloth?'

'It was dark—'

'It was dark when she gave you the stick?' Philip stayed with his mouth open.

'Was it?' pressed Enwright.

'Yes,' said Philip.

'Right. She told you the lights had fused?'

'Yes.'

'And that was the reason you didn't try and switch one on, was it?'

'Yes. There was always light in the hall from the Avenue lamps. There are two windows and a fan-light.'

'Who did you see in the hall?'

'No one. The body was on the floor then.'

'Well, Mr. Stanley, that seems to settle what we want to know. It is a pity so much time has been wasted.'

2

In the witness box, Sebastian was confused. He could not remember which night had been which, as all had been so much alike. The judge's efforts to help him made things worse.

Philip listened in a state of tense anger. He knew when the old man was acting, and nobody else seemed to. He appeared as a doddery old fool, sharp but easily confused.

When Enwright asked him if he usually admitted visitors in the middle of the night he went wild.

158

'Why not? Any time! They were all trying to kill me. Ball, Philip, my housekeeper—all of them, plotting to get rid of me. I knew it! I watched it! I heard it! It was meant to be me not Ball, lying there dead. Me! Ball was never in it. It was all against me! He was unlucky. He must have got in the way. It was me, all of them, all of them! I could—'

Enwright gave up. Sebastian left, labelled mad as a hatter, as indeed, the magistrates' court had decided not so long before. Philip's face was grey.

Med made a great impression. She looked magnificent and splendid in her defence of the old man's peculiarities. It was clear to anyone but Philip that her life was devoted to looking after the poor old fellow in his fading years.

Then the crunch came when Enwright asked, 'Were you having an affair with the prisoner?'

'With *him* do you mean?' She looked astonished. 'Do you think I would?'

'Did you sleep with my client at any time?'

'I'll be damned if I would.'

'He states that you did.'

'He is givin' himself one of those illusions of grandness or whatever it is. I have no time for him and for certain not in my bed.'

'Did you not arrange to see him the night that Ball was killed?'

'I'd see him comin' first. That is, no, sir.'

The question which shook the jury was that

159

put by the Prosecution.

'Did he ever mention to you that he had some idea of murdering his uncle?'

'For sure he did.'

'What did you say to that?'

'I laughed. Why 'tis a fine joke when a man with less guts than a pair of garters starts talkin' about doin' somebody in. No, I could never take such a thing seriously, or I'd be callin' the police, I tell you that.'

Of course, the splendid woman was defending the old man, and of course she would call the police. She was a fine woman, no doubt of that.

'What did you think when he said that?' Prosecution went on.

'Well, I had the choice of thinkin' whether he was jokin' or was off his nut. Either way it was not funny to my way of thinkin'.'

The police case had all along been kept to the insane jealousy of the ineffectual and frustrated attacking another man he had fancied had succeeded where he had failed.

Med's denial of any affair helped this right on. Sebastian's declaration that everybody was always trying to kill him had laughed any such suggestion out of court.

Any attempt at that stage to implicate Med was going to be given the jaundiced eye by the jury, and as it could prove nothing Enwright sat on it.

But Enwright's appearance was, as ever,

160

impressive and persuasive and he was more relieved than surprised when it was found that the jury could not agree.

A new trial was ordered and the jury dismissed. Time passed.

The trouble with the case was that it was so plain, so simple, so easily explained. Philip had stayed on at Fairfield because of his infatuation. There had been no other reason, it seemed. He had found Ball that night, and, fancying the man was going upstairs, had caused a struggle, death and an unlucky trip which kept the murderer where he least wanted to be.

Sebastian had phoned the police because he had heard noises downstairs, noises of a fight. All this had come up in such a natural way that the jury must have expected each step of the drama.

But Enwright did not like simplicity. Where he found it he suspected complications hidden behind. He saw Philip again.

'From the time when you began your stay at this house a kind of serial charade of wild scenes between Ball and your uncle was enacted for your special benefit night after night?'

'I've told you all that.'

'But the night before the last there were two visitors. First Watson, the policeman who was also first on the scene the following night, then the woman detective. Both these people came as would-be protectors of Ball's safety.'

It was then for the first time that Philip said, 'No, she came to take the business offer instead of Ball.'

'Take the business offer? We know now there wasn't one.'

'There must have been something. That was what she said, I'm sure. It would be to protect Ball, of course, so it amounts to the same thing.'

'The continued charade of violence has intrigued me from the start of this case, but it seems not to have led anywhere. The only purpose of it I could conceive was that it would, at some later date, have persuaded you to give evidence that extreme bad feeling existed between the two men. In the event that evidence would have played more against you than anyone else. Was there any other odd activity in the house while you were there?'

'It was all odd. But there was one thing. He used to sneak up into the attic at night and she got me to follow him up there and see what he was up to. It was all part of a game, I think now. Sort of nerve game.'

'Did she give a reason for you following?'

'Yes. She thought he had a lot of money hidden up there. But when he got up there he just pretended to disappear. It was a game on her to stop her being nosy.'

'I don't see how that could affect the case. It's the squabbling show that intrigues—'

'He laughed at me! He did! Ball! The night I fell into the door—no, she did that. Shoved me. She did that twice. She's very strong. Can sort of aim you—'

'Ball laughed at you? During one of these shouting games?'

'I interrupted one. It was the night after the detectives called. Ball turned up in the middle of the night. That night. He helped me into the room and he was laughing at me.'

'Are you sure?' Enwright stared.

'They were all laughing at me all the time,' Philip said in sudden anger. 'I know that now. From the time I turned up there they made a game of it. There was nothing up in the attics, there was no business deal, there was no fight between Ball and uncle or any blackmail on Med. There was nothing except a game, and I was the monkey on a stick.'

'To drive you mad or make you lose your temper and do something they wanted?'

'I don't know because it didn't happen. But I don't know why Ball's dead. The way he laughed I thought he was in it with them.'

'Why didn't you give these details before?'

'I didn't care before. I just thought I hadn't got a hope. I've changed my mind now . . . I suppose the police did question Uncle and Med at the time?'

'Of course. But you seemed to be caught in the act. And you tied yourself up so with lies. That's always a bad thing.'

'I didn't know the half. I didn't know Ball only started to be frightened of violence after I got there. I see now it was part of the game, and it's nearly fixed me, but I didn't know that till the trial.'

'It didn't come out till then. Detective Watson said it in the witness box. I complained about it, you remember, but it did no good.'

'Will they give the same case next time?'

'Yes. Plus, of course, anything else that may be found in the meantime.'

The case was tried again and after a five hour dispute the jury returned a verdict of not guilty. Philip was set free of the court but imprisoned in his mind.

3

For many weeks he suffered a severe mental depression. He felt he had been wrecked. He became frightened of everything, and if he went out, drank alone, came back alone and sank into a grey despair.

After a long time he began to realise that he was suffering from a mental disease, and the cause was Fairfield and the two people in it.

That idea grew more and more important. He saw that until those sores were removed from his mind there was no escape for him.

So on the night of January the fifteenth he went back through the dripping mist to the house, by the garden way, as he had done before. This time he had a pistol in his pocket.

For some time he stood near the back door, listening to the steady dripping of wet from the trees. Curiously, it seemed all like the first time. So like, even the old motive returned, the taking of Sebastian's money in place of a feeling of a desperate necessity to get rid of those two people.

He went to the door and tried the handle. The door pushed in. He held it, gripped by a fear that this was too easy. The moment passed. He remembered what he had been through and opened the door.

He used his torch. He laid it on the kitchen table and buttoned his gloves to make sure they did not come off. He picked up the torch, drew the pistol from his pocket and went out into the hall.

It was all as before, the green light coming through the hall from the Avenue, but as he crossed the wide hall he saw a strip of yellow light under the study door.

His heart beat fast. He went to the door, put the torch in his pocket then opened the door suddenly. Sebastian was standing by the safe and did not look round.

'Go to bed!' Sebastian said.

Philip raised the gun and aimed at the old man's back. As he fired his arm was gripped from behind and he was half turned back towards the door.

165

They heard the bullet scream after it hit the safe. Med let Philip go. They both looked down the room to Sebastian.

Sebastian turned slowly towards them, and as he did they could not see his features for blood streaming down them. He stayed like that, it seemed, for whole minutes, and then he collapsed quite suddenly and lay still on the rug.

'Give me the gun,' she said.

He let her take it from him and stood there while she went to Sebastian.

'He's dead,' she said. 'Come here. Quick!'

Under her directions they carried him halfway back to where Philip had fired, then put him down before any blood had stained the carpet. She put the gun in Sebastian's hand so that the dead fingers mauled it all over, did both hands, and finally made his right hand hold the gun and trigger.

Sweat poured down Philip's face as he watched. She finished and got up.

'Come to bed,' she said. 'You'd better.'

They went out and she closed the door carefully. They went up into the bedroom, where no lights were on, just the green glow from the Avenue patterning the ceiling.

'So you did it at last,' she said. 'That was sheer luck. You weren't aiming right anyhow. Sheer luck it just came back off the safe, and you've got a good, drunken shooting accident.'

'Was he drunk?'

166

'It got regular after you went. Every damn night.'

He went to the window.

'I meant—' he began.

'I know what you meant. Some people aren't ever grateful. I've saved you twice, remember. Twice at your trials. Now this is the third time. Better not think of killin' me after that.'

He stayed staring out of the window, until he heard an old familiar creak and shuffle upstairs.

'It's still there!' he said.

'Rats,' she said. 'I found that out. It's rats up there. And another little thing I found, too. Some damn long time ago he murdered a girl here and under a floor up there there's the skeleton still. He was always lucky, your uncle—until Ball found out.

'Ball found out just before you came. That was the deal they were always on about. Ball was quotin' the price he wanted for the next instalment. It was he who was boss. You didn't think that, did you?'

'Why didn't you say? At the trial? You'd have been safe! Sebastian killed him and you knew the reason, you—'

'He wanted to get you so you'd do it for him. And the way he'd fixed it you as good as did it without doin' it, if you know what I mean. He was a good fixer.'

'But why didn't you say?'

167

'Because he had a hold on me. He had a big, strong, nasty hold, and I'll tell you this, darlin', there's nothin' worse in this life than to be ruled by somebody that's got a big, strong, nasty hold on you.'

And she laughed.

We hope you have enjoyed this Large Print book. Other Chivers Press or Thorndike Press Large Print books are available at your library or directly from the publishers.

For more information about current and forthcoming titles, please call or write, without obligation, to:

Chivers Large Print
published by BBC Audiobooks Ltd
St James House, The Square
Lower Bristol Road
Bath BA2 3BH
UK
email: bbcaudiobooks@bbc.co.uk
www.bbcaudiobooks.co.uk

OR

Thorndike Press
295 Kennedy Memorial Drive
Waterville
Maine 04901
USA
www.gale.com/thorndike
www.gale.com/wheeler

All our Large Print titles are designed for easy reading, and all our books are made to last.